W9-BMO-654

MANGA MATH MYSTERIES

THE LOST KEY

A Mystery with Whole Numbers

by Melinda Thielbar

illustrated by Tintin Pantoja

#1

GRAPHIC UNIVERSE™ • MINNEAPOLIS • NEW YORK

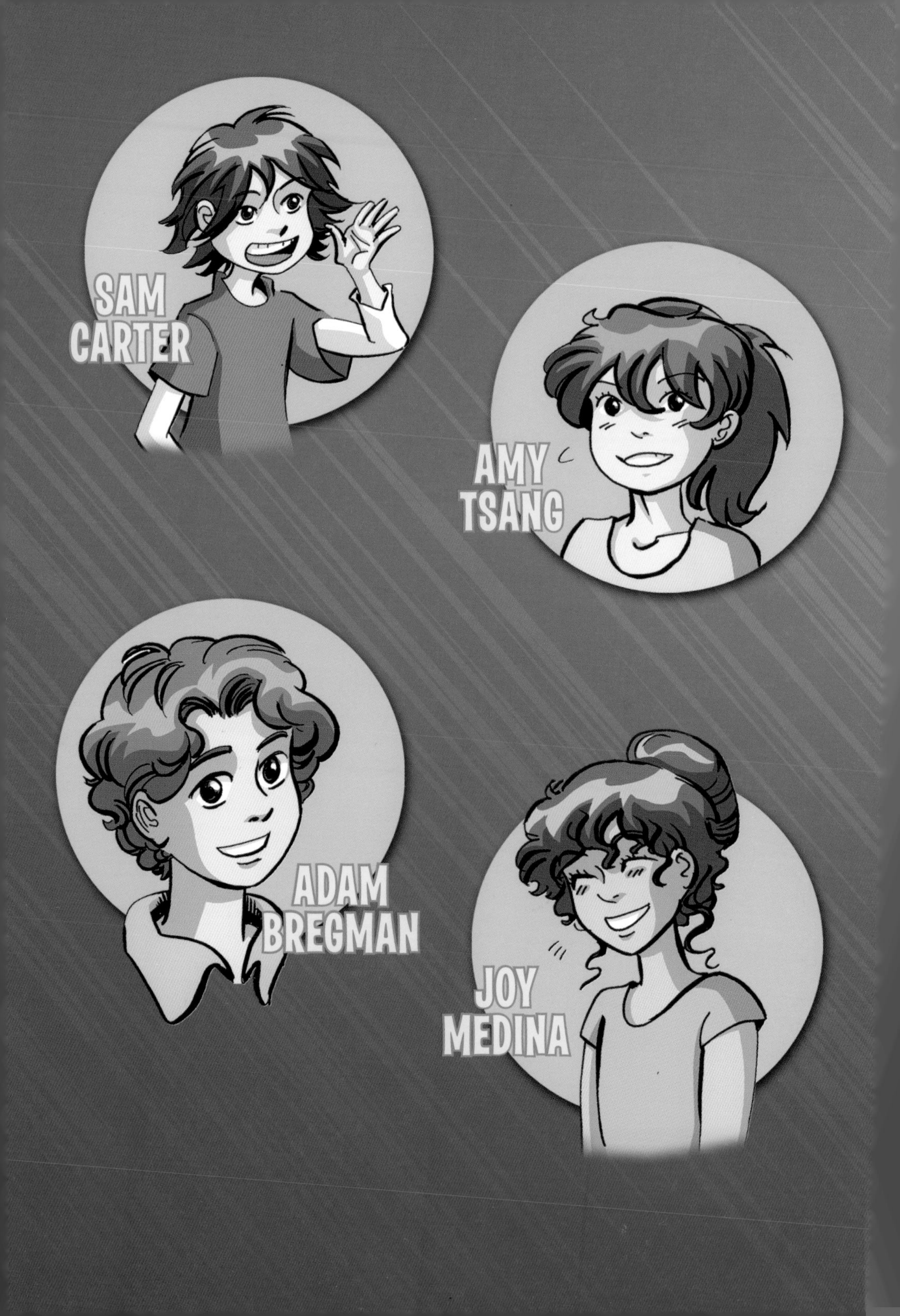
SAM CARTER
AMY TSANG
ADAM BREGMAN
JOY MEDINA

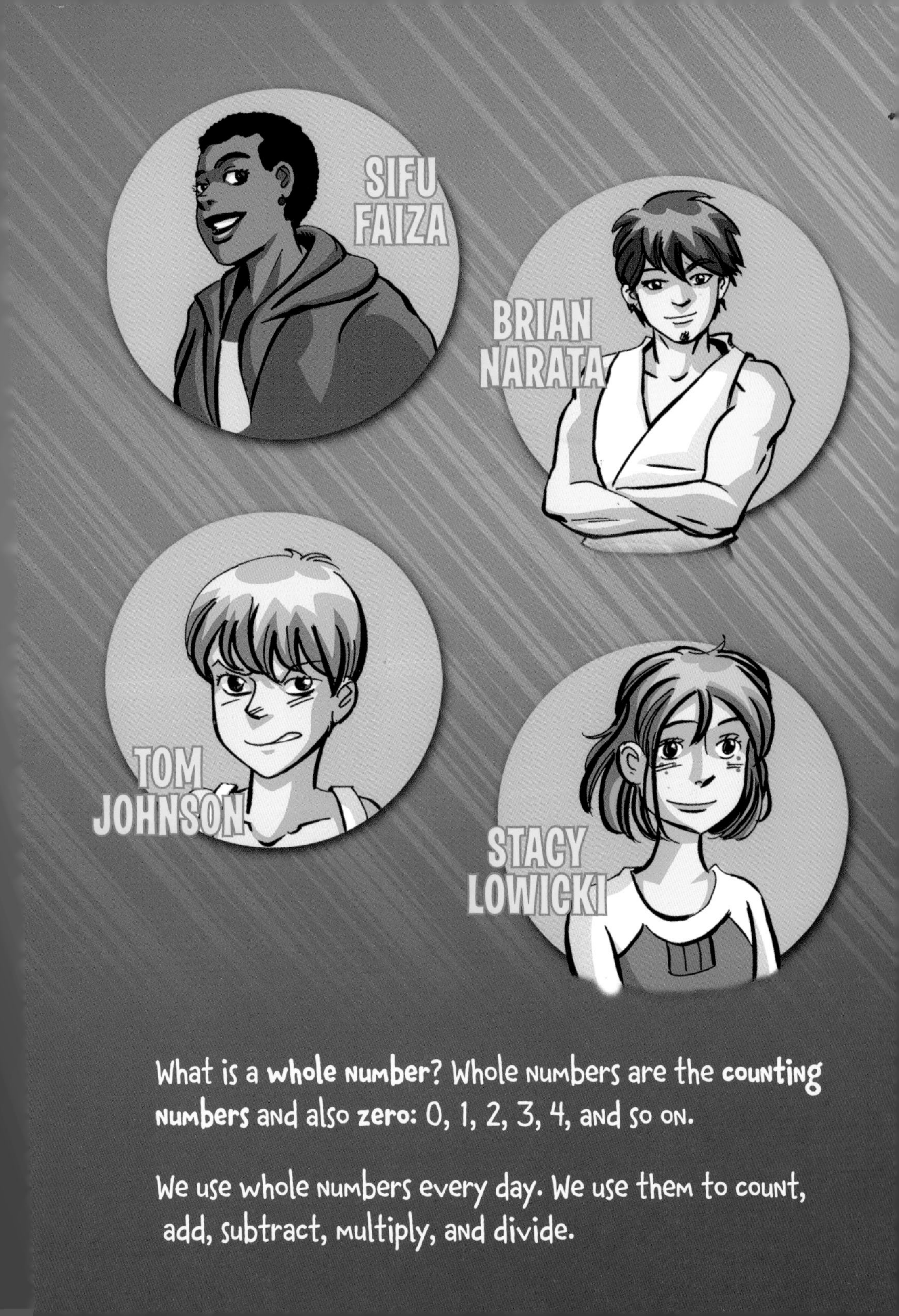
SIFU FAIZA
BRIAN NARATA
TOM JOHNSON
STACY LOWICKI

What is a **whole number**? Whole numbers are the **counting numbers** and also **zero:** 0, 1, 2, 3, 4, and so on.

We use whole numbers every day. We use them to count, add, subtract, multiply, and divide.

Story by Melinda Thielbar
Pencils and inks by Tintin Pantoja
Coloring by Hi-Fi Design
Lettering by Marshall Dillon

Graphic Universe™
A division of Lerner Publishing Group, Inc.
241 First Avenue North
Minneapolis, MN 55401 U.S.A.

Website address: www.lernerbooks.com

Library of Congress Cataloging-in-Publication Data

Thielbar, Melinda.
    The lost key : a mystery with whole numbers / story by Melinda Thielbar ; art by
Tintin Pantoja.
        p. cm. — (Manga math mysteries)
    Summary: When equipment is stolen from Sifu Faiza's Kung Fu School, where
students learn compassion and responsibility as they train their minds and bodies,
four friends use basic math skills to track down the culprits.
    ISBN: 978-0-7613-3853-6 (lib. bdg. : alk. paper)
    1. Graphic novels. [1. Graphic novels. 2. Mystery and detective stories. 3.
Mathematics—Fiction. 4. Kung fu—Fiction. 5. Schools—Fiction.] I. Pantoja, Tintin,
ill. II. Title.
PZ7.7.T48Lo 2010
741.5'973—dc22   2008053242

Manufactured in the United States of America
1 2 3 4 5 6 – DP – 15 14 13 12 11 10

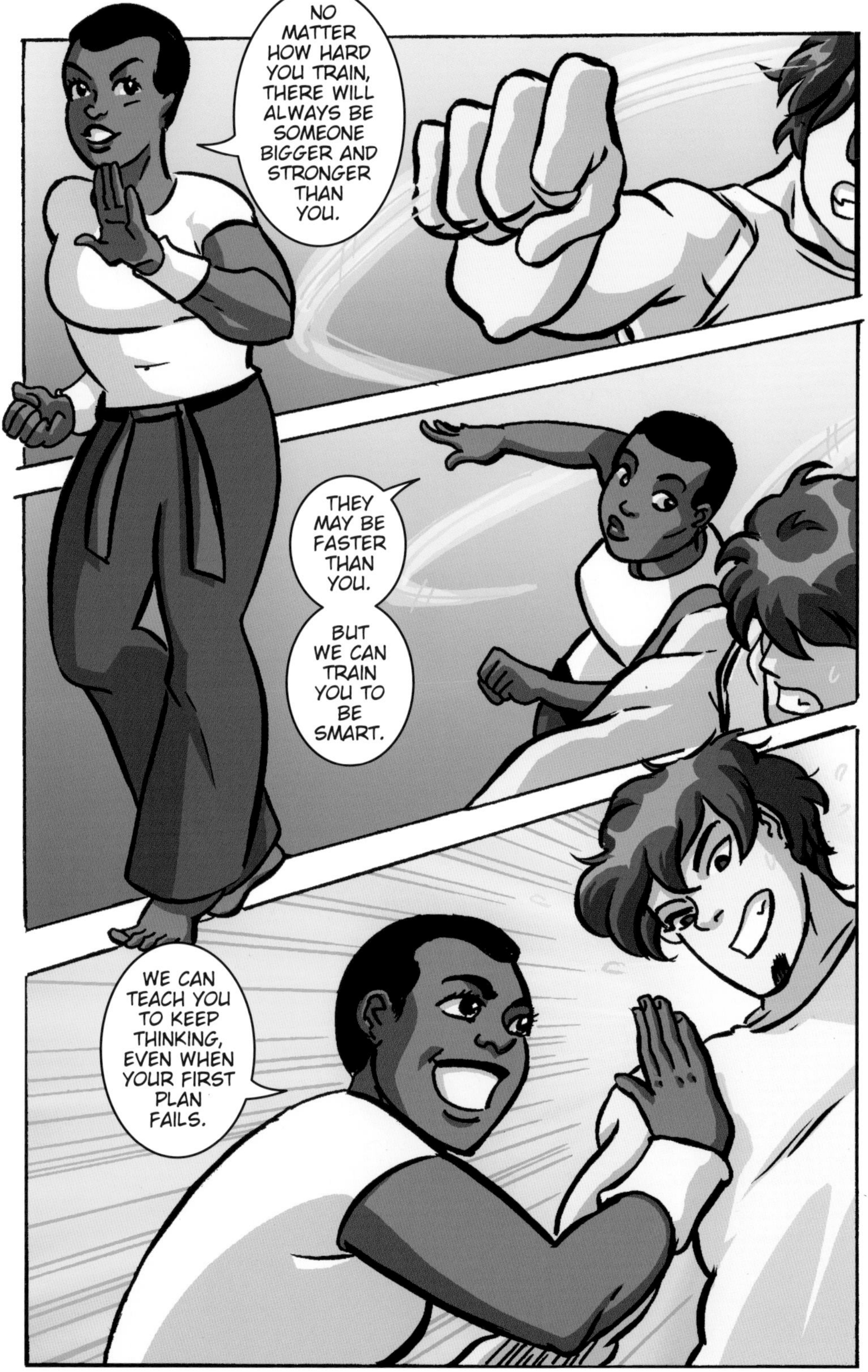
NO MATTER HOW HARD YOU TRAIN, THERE WILL ALWAYS BE SOMEONE BIGGER AND STRONGER THAN YOU.
THEY MAY BE FASTER THAN YOU.
BUT WE CAN TRAIN YOU TO BE SMART.
WE CAN TEACH YOU TO KEEP THINKING, EVEN WHEN YOUR FIRST PLAN FAILS.

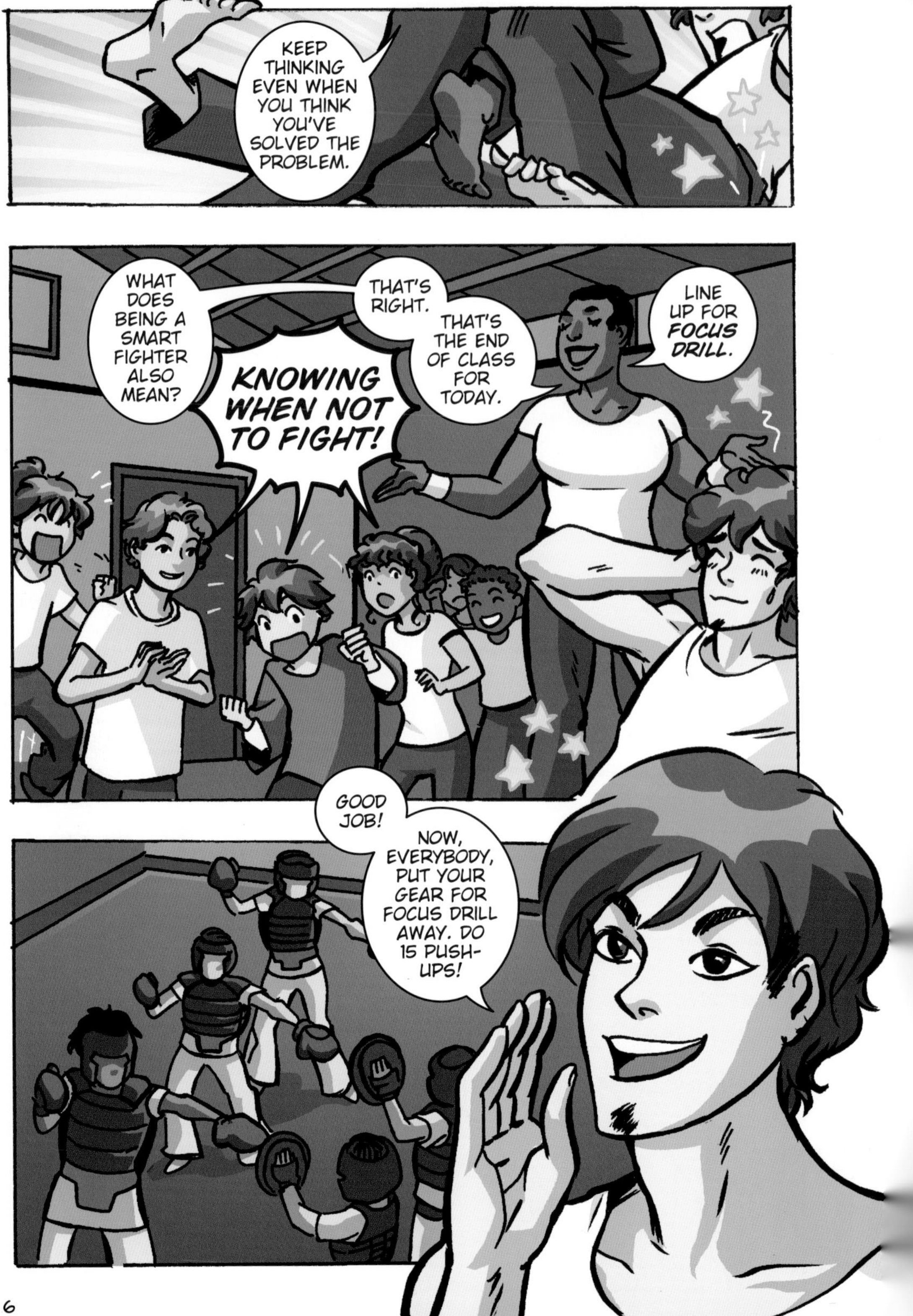
KEEP THINKING EVEN WHEN YOU THINK YOU'VE SOLVED THE PROBLEM.
WHAT DOES BEING A SMART FIGHTER ALSO MEAN?
KNOWING WHEN NOT TO FIGHT!
THAT'S RIGHT.
THAT'S THE END OF CLASS FOR TODAY.
LINE UP FOR FOCUS DRILL.
GOOD JOB!
NOW, EVERYBODY, PUT YOUR GEAR FOR FOCUS DRILL AWAY. DO 15 PUSH-UPS!

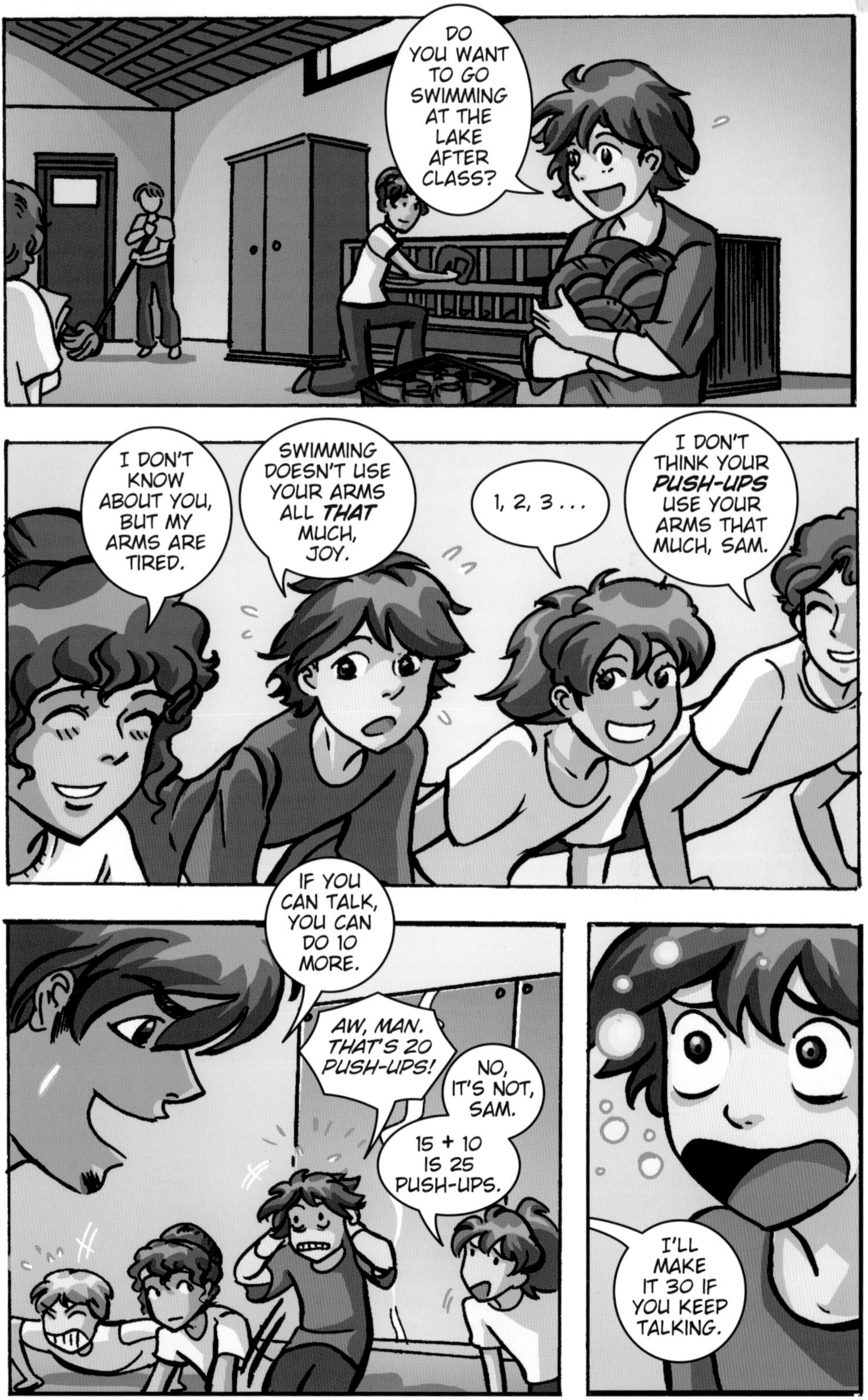
DO YOU WANT TO GO SWIMMING AT THE LAKE AFTER CLASS?
I DON'T KNOW ABOUT YOU, BUT MY ARMS ARE TIRED.
SWIMMING DOESN'T USE YOUR ARMS ALL *THAT* MUCH, JOY.
1, 2, 3 . . .
I DON'T THINK YOUR *PUSH-UPS* USE YOUR ARMS THAT MUCH, SAM.
IF YOU CAN TALK, YOU CAN DO 10 MORE.
AW, MAN. THAT'S 20 PUSH-UPS!
NO, IT'S NOT, SAM.
15 + 10 IS 25 PUSH-UPS.
I'LL MAKE IT 30 IF YOU KEEP TALKING.

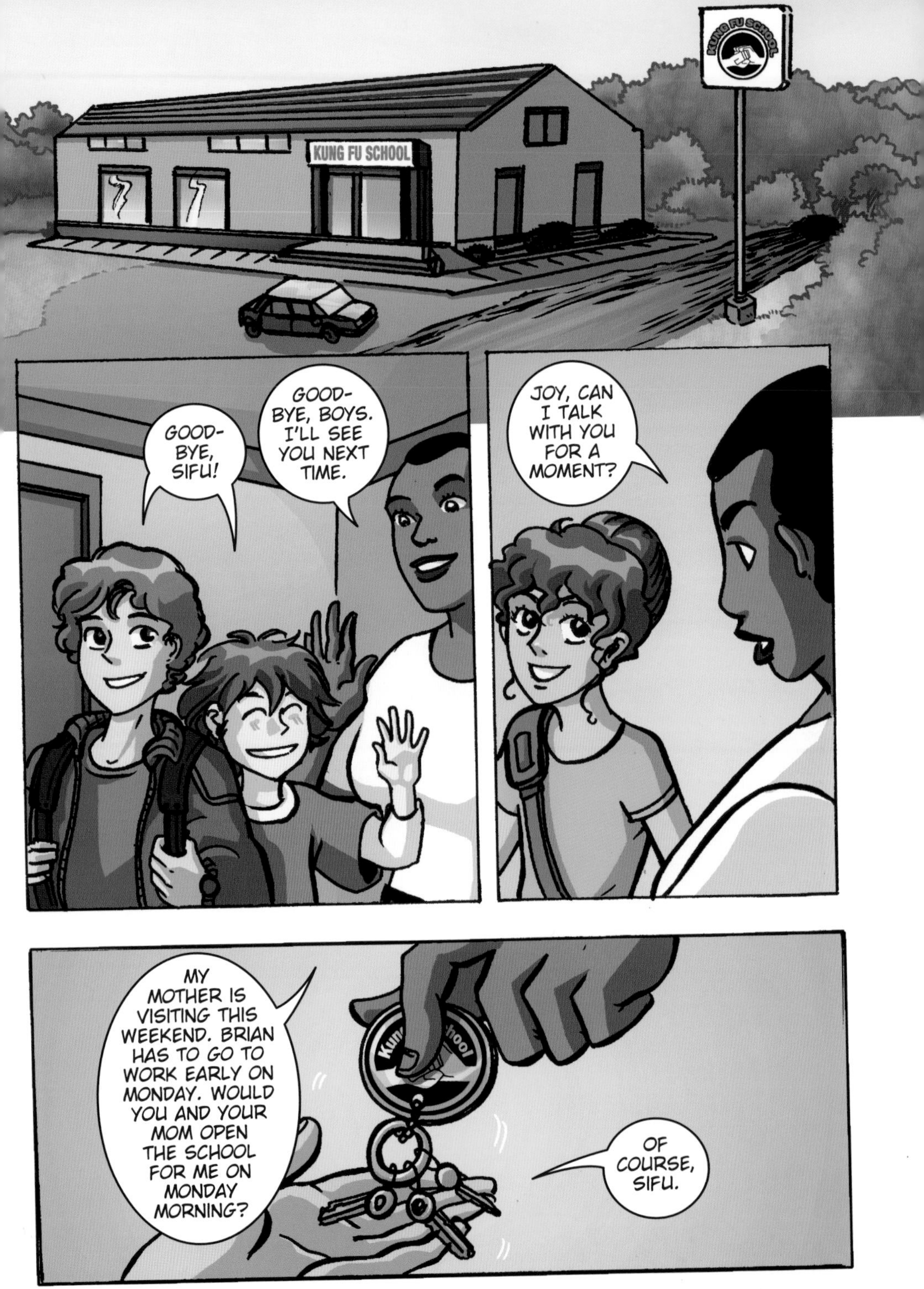
KUNG FU SCHOOL
KUNG FU SCHOOL
GOOD-BYE, SIFU!
GOOD-BYE, BOYS. I'LL SEE YOU NEXT TIME.
JOY, CAN I TALK WITH YOU FOR A MOMENT?
MY MOTHER IS VISITING THIS WEEKEND. BRIAN HAS TO GO TO WORK EARLY ON MONDAY. WOULD YOU AND YOUR MOM OPEN THE SCHOOL FOR ME ON MONDAY MORNING?
OF COURSE, SIFU.

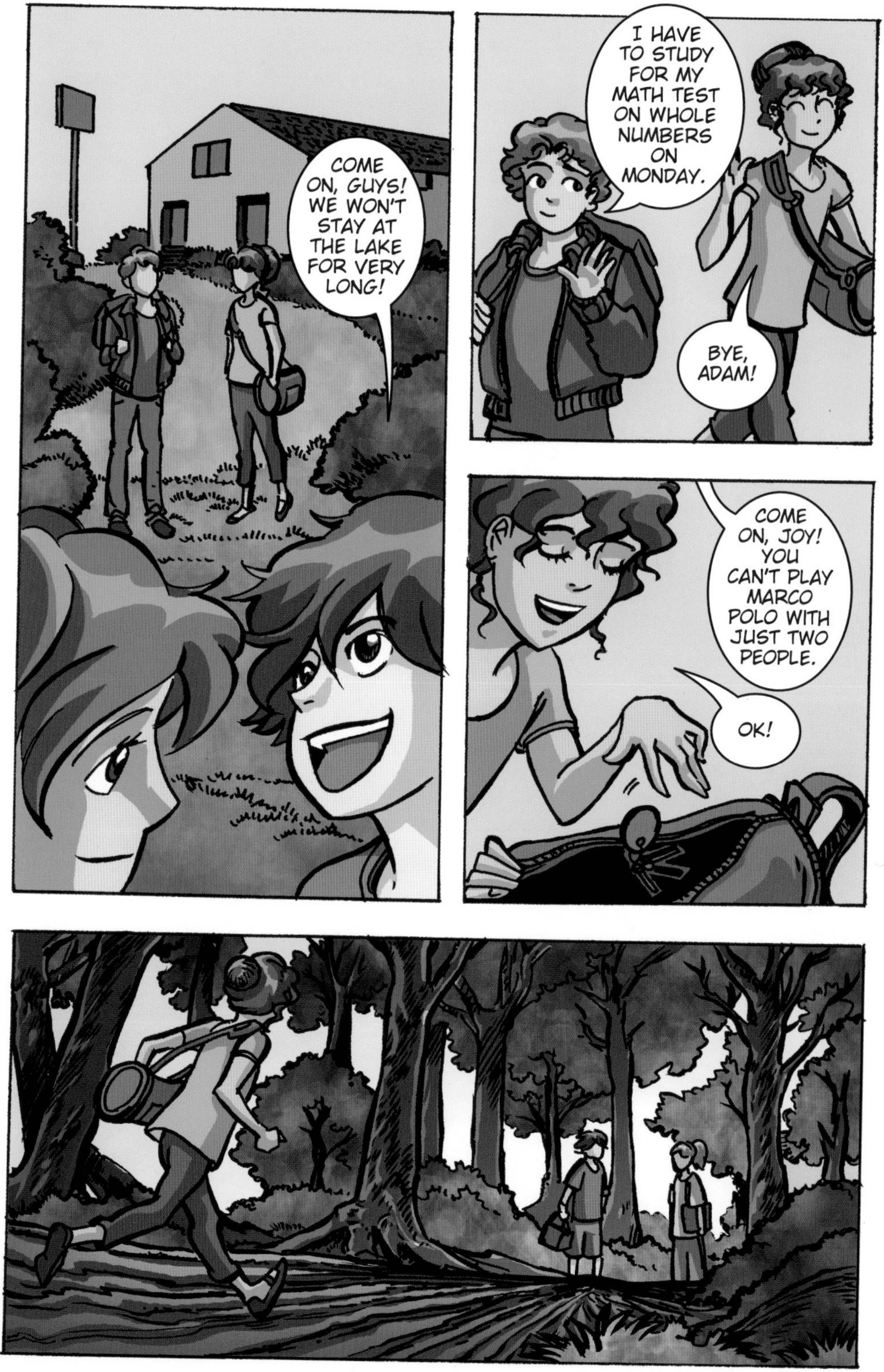
COME ON, GUYS! WE WON'T STAY AT THE LAKE FOR VERY LONG!
I HAVE TO STUDY FOR MY MATH TEST ON WHOLE NUMBERS ON MONDAY.
BYE, ADAM!
COME ON, JOY! YOU CAN'T PLAY MARCO POLO WITH JUST TWO PEOPLE.
OK!

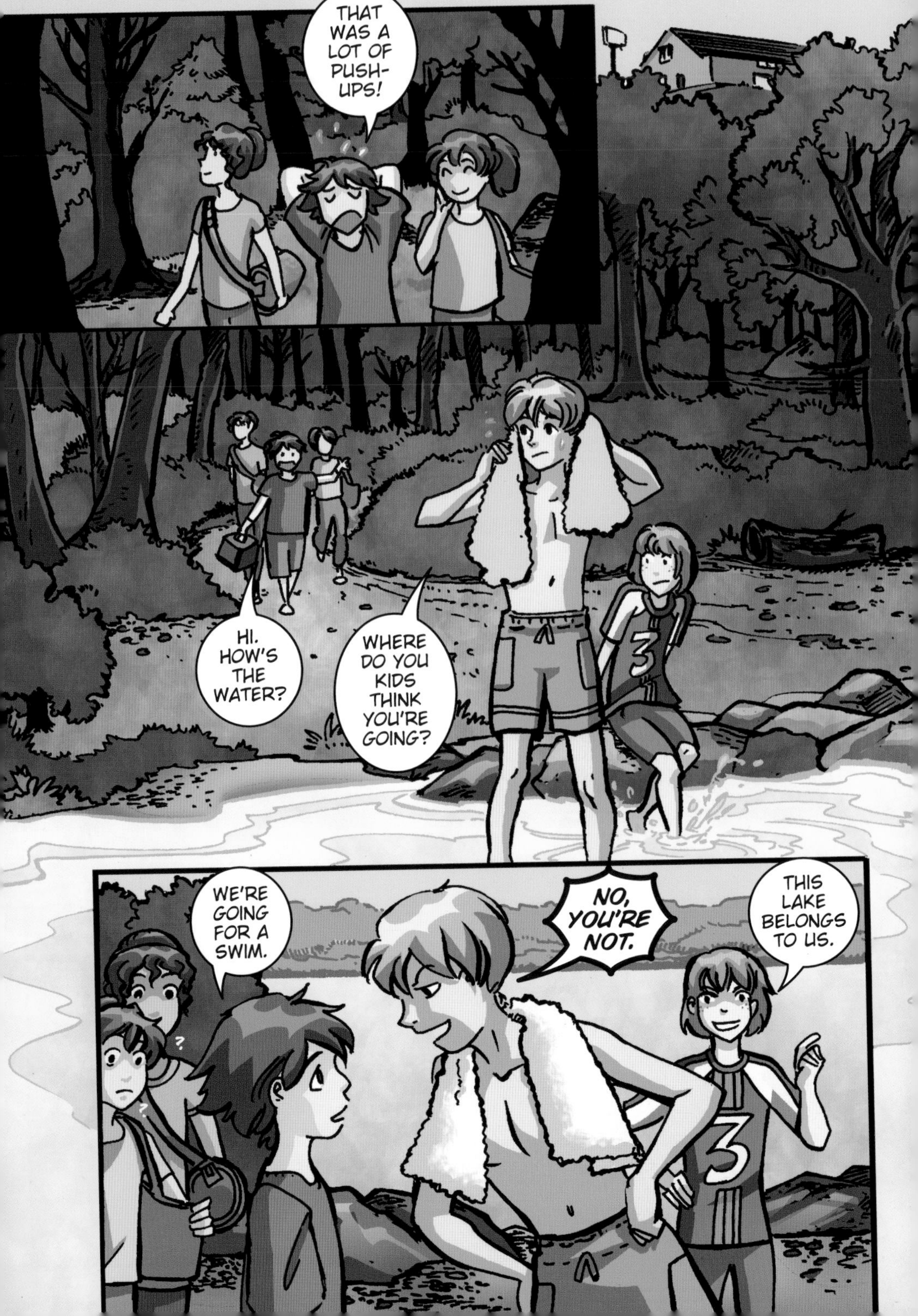
THAT WAS A LOT OF PUSH-UPS!
HI. HOW'S THE WATER?
WHERE DO YOU KIDS THINK YOU'RE GOING?
WE'RE GOING FOR A SWIM.
NO, YOU'RE NOT.
THIS LAKE BELONGS TO US.

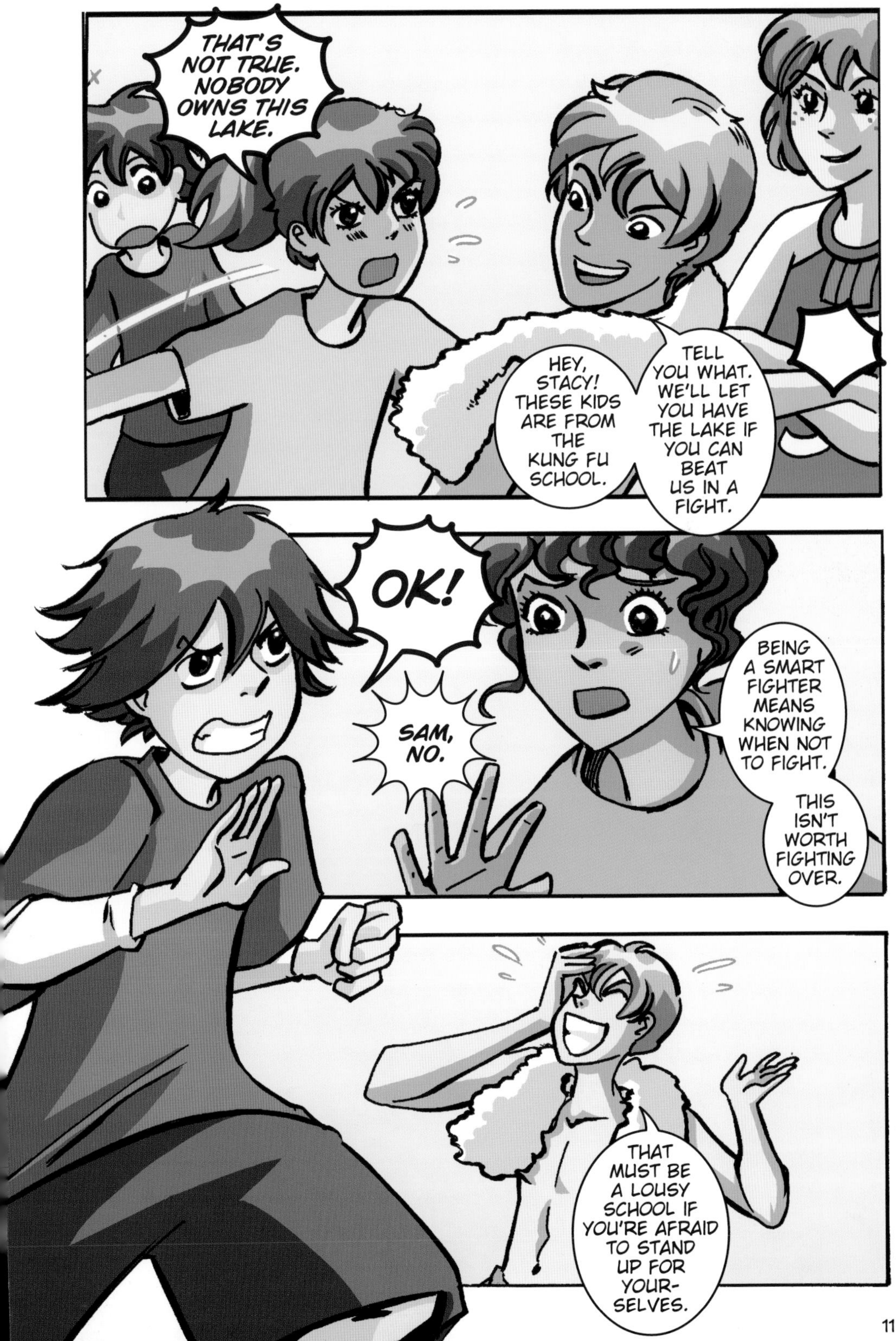
THAT'S NOT TRUE. NOBODY OWNS THIS LAKE.
HEY, STACY! THESE KIDS ARE FROM THE KUNG FU SCHOOL.
TELL YOU WHAT. WE'LL LET YOU HAVE THE LAKE IF YOU CAN BEAT US IN A FIGHT.
OK!
SAM, NO.
BEING A SMART FIGHTER MEANS KNOWING WHEN NOT TO FIGHT.
THIS ISN'T WORTH FIGHTING OVER.
THAT MUST BE A LOUSY SCHOOL IF YOU'RE AFRAID TO STAND UP FOR YOURSELVES.

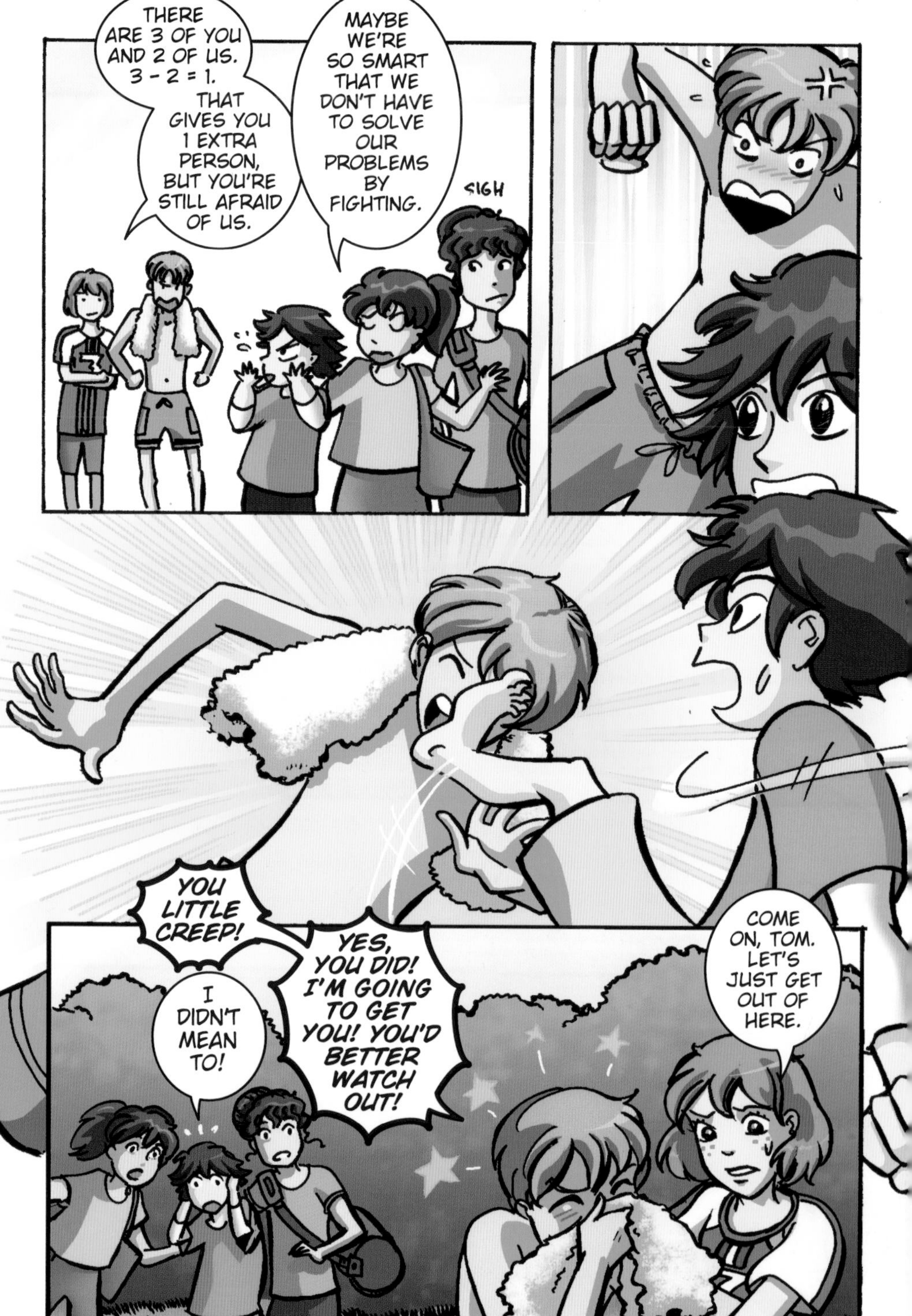
THERE ARE 3 OF YOU AND 2 OF US. 3 - 2 = 1. THAT GIVES YOU 1 EXTRA PERSON, BUT YOU'RE STILL AFRAID OF US.
MAYBE WE'RE SO SMART THAT WE DON'T HAVE TO SOLVE OUR PROBLEMS BY FIGHTING.
SIGH
YOU LITTLE CREEP!
I DIDN'T MEAN TO!
YES, YOU DID! I'M GOING TO GET YOU! YOU'D BETTER WATCH OUT!
COME ON, TOM. LET'S JUST GET OUT OF HERE.

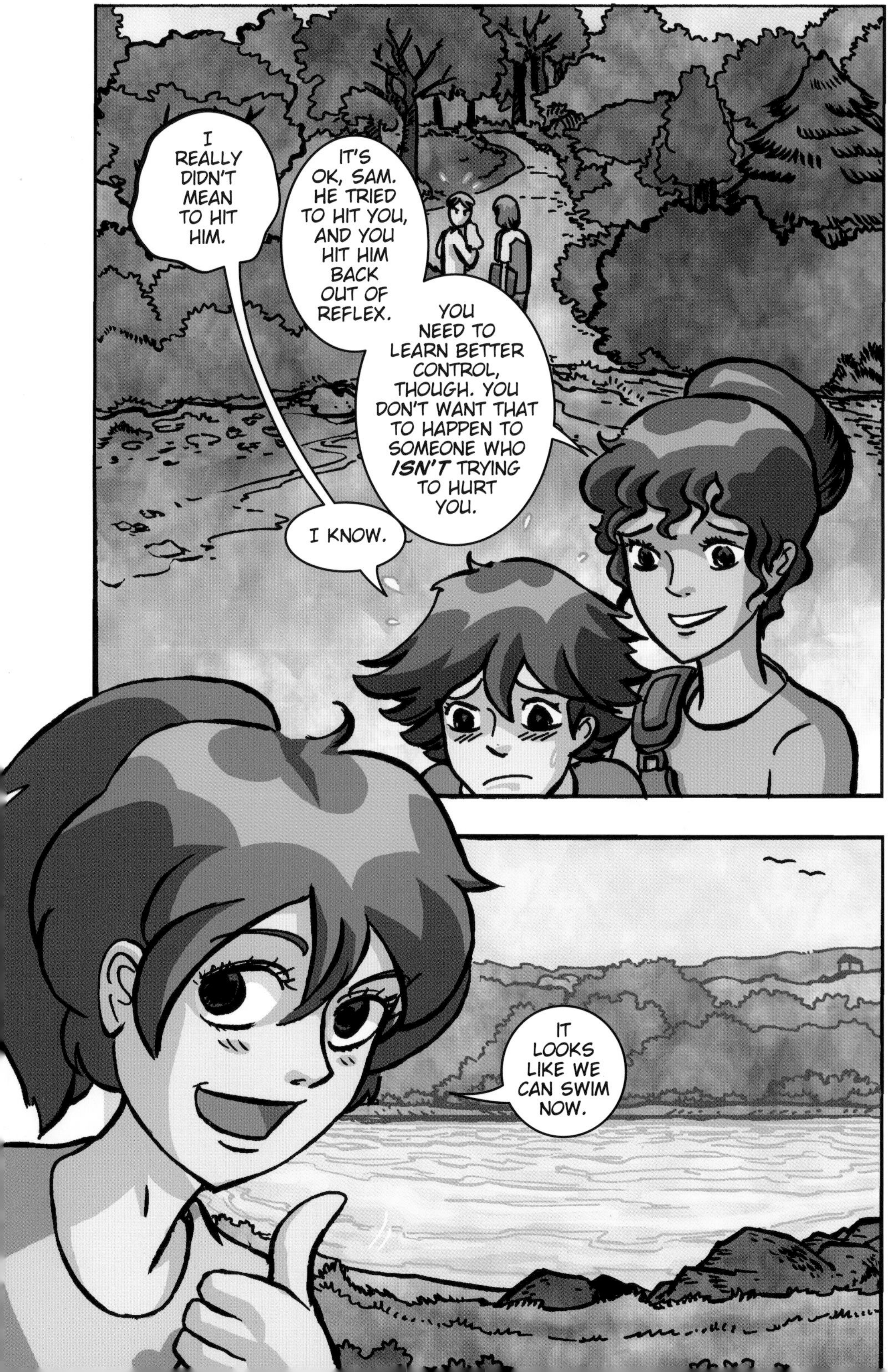
I REALLY DIDN'T MEAN TO HIT HIM.
IT'S OK, SAM. HE TRIED TO HIT YOU, AND YOU HIT HIM BACK OUT OF REFLEX.
YOU NEED TO LEARN BETTER CONTROL, THOUGH. YOU DON'T WANT THAT TO HAPPEN TO SOMEONE WHO *ISN'T* TRYING TO HURT YOU.
I KNOW.
IT LOOKS LIKE WE CAN SWIM NOW.

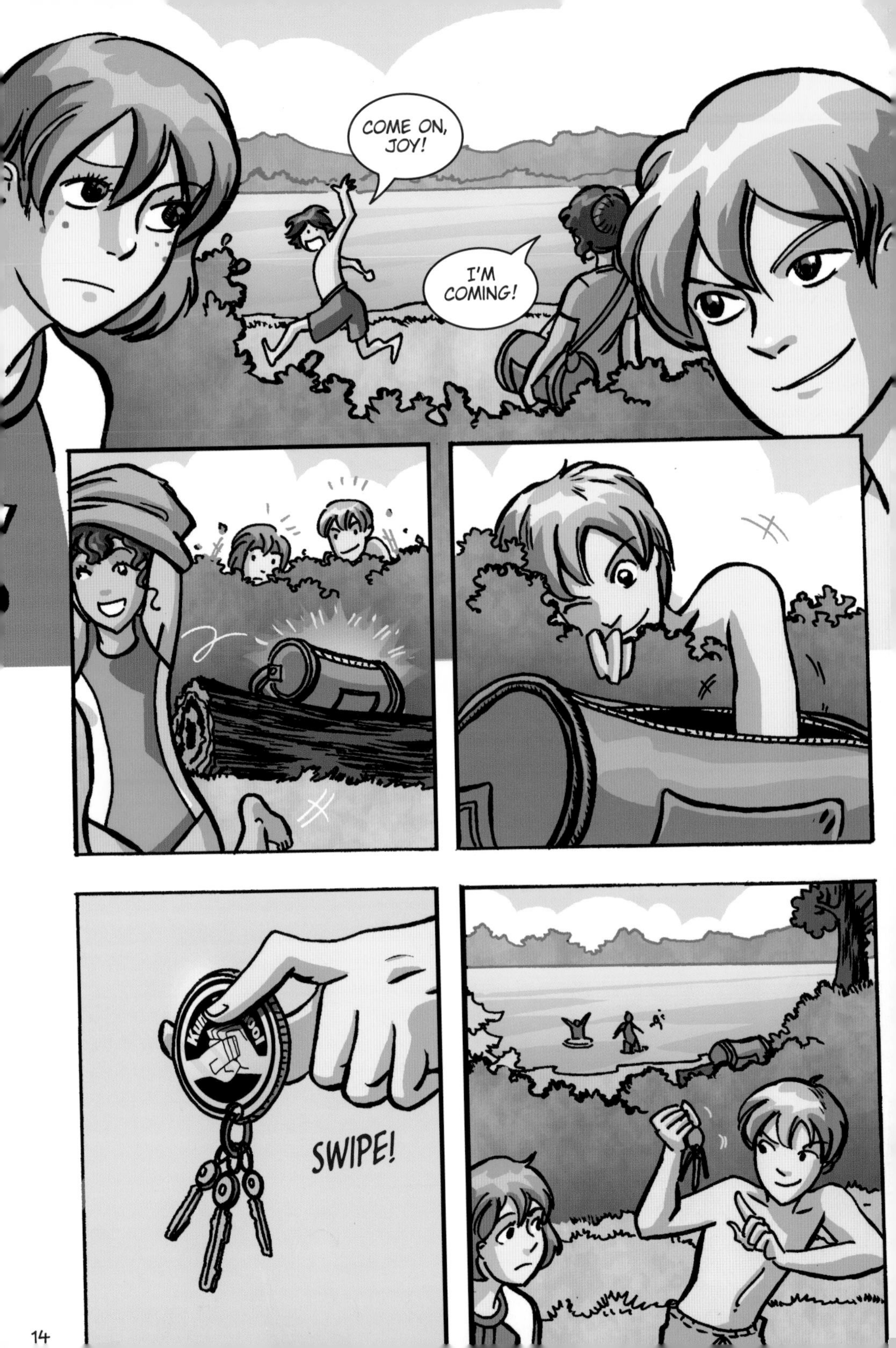
COME ON, JOY!
I'M COMING!
SWIPE!

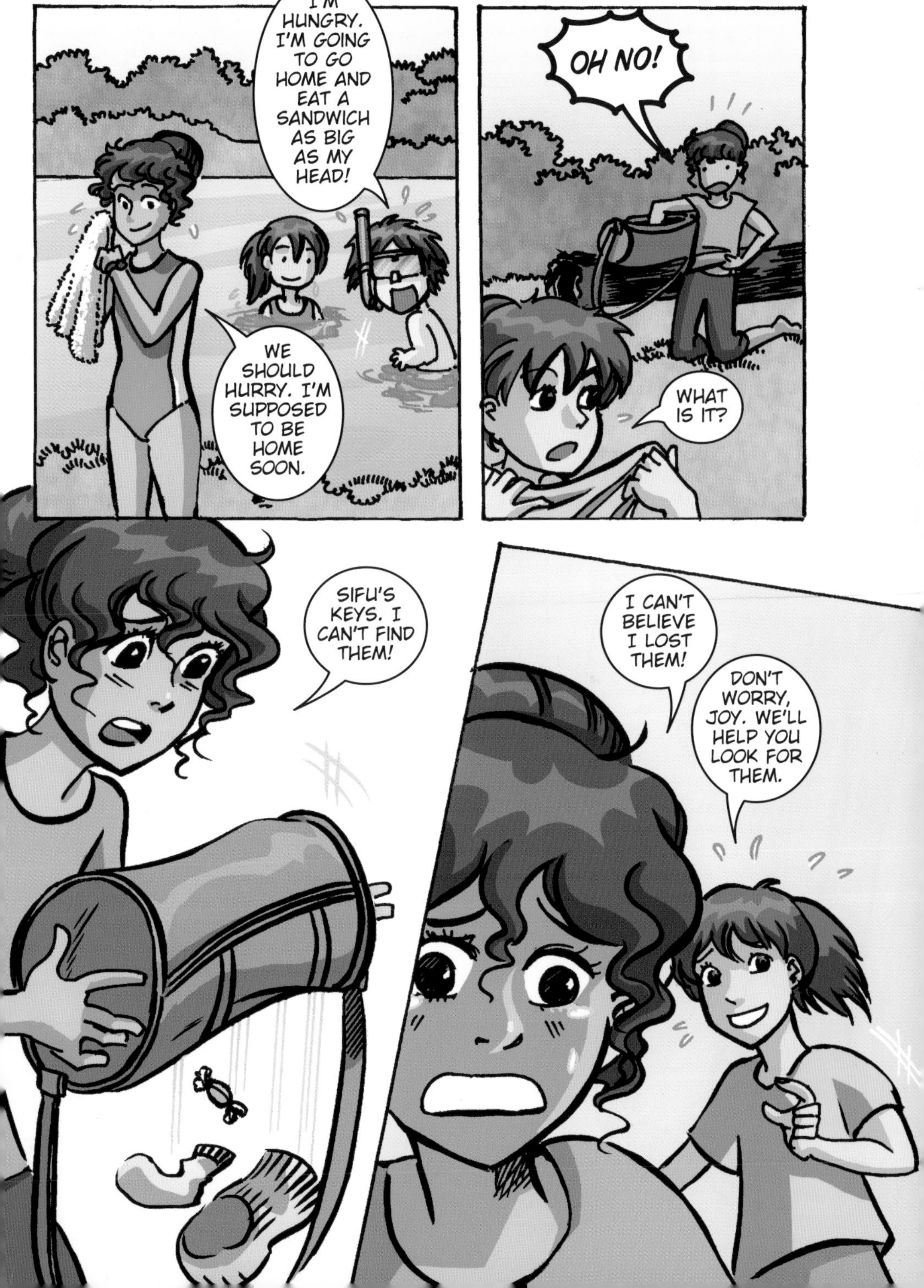
I'M HUNGRY. I'M GOING TO GO HOME AND EAT A SANDWICH AS BIG AS MY HEAD!
WE SHOULD HURRY. I'M SUPPOSED TO BE HOME SOON.
OH NO!
WHAT IS IT?
SIFU'S KEYS. I CAN'T FIND THEM!
I CAN'T BELIEVE I LOST THEM!
DON'T WORRY, JOY. WE'LL HELP YOU LOOK FOR THEM.

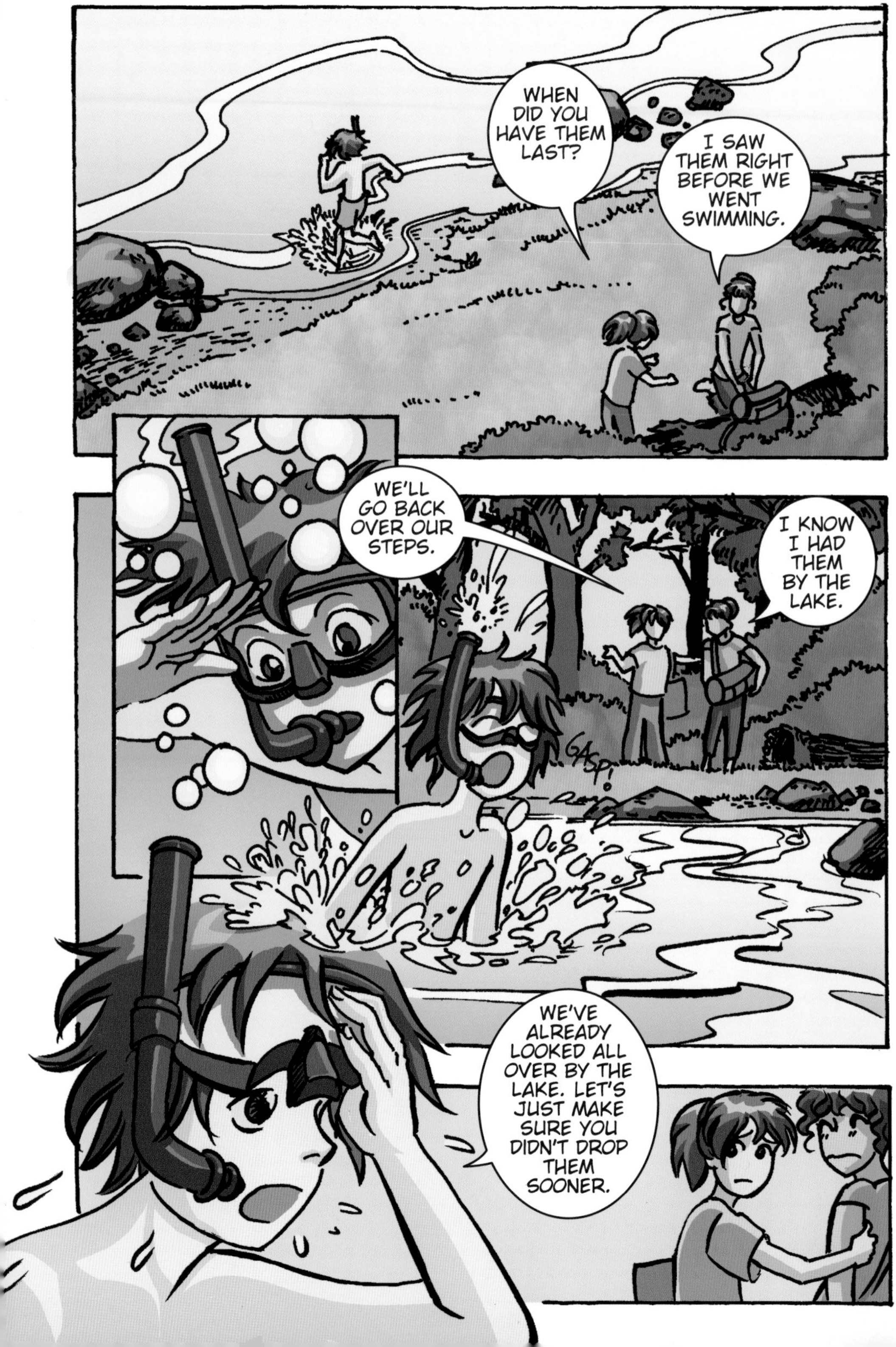
WHEN DID YOU HAVE THEM LAST?
I SAW THEM RIGHT BEFORE WE WENT SWIMMING.
WE'LL GO BACK OVER OUR STEPS.
I KNOW I HAD THEM BY THE LAKE.
GASP!
WE'VE ALREADY LOOKED ALL OVER BY THE LAKE. LET'S JUST MAKE SURE YOU DIDN'T DROP THEM SOONER.

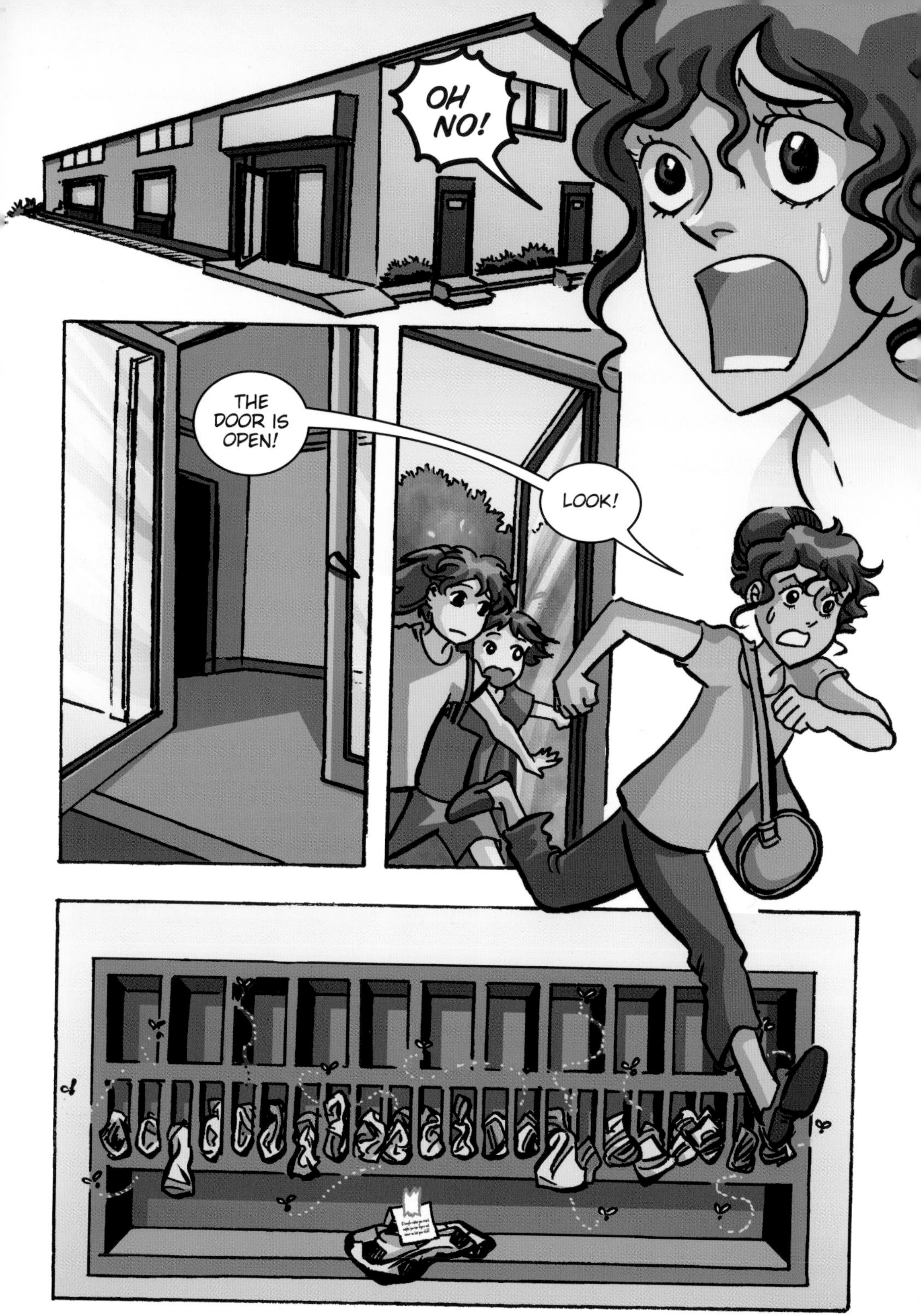
OH NO!
THE DOOR IS OPEN!
LOOK!

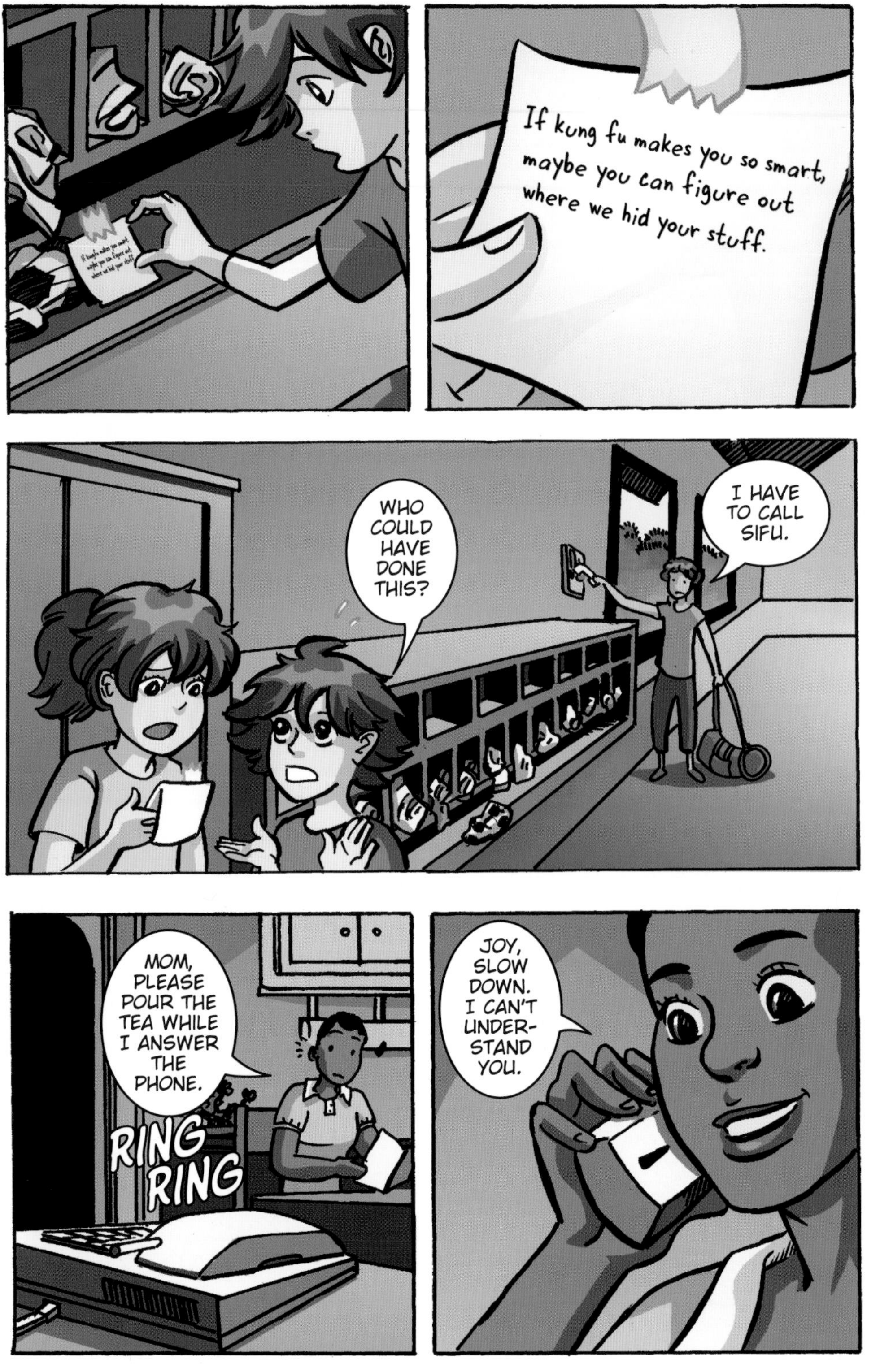
If kung fu makes you so smart, maybe you can figure out where we hid your stuff.
WHO COULD HAVE DONE THIS?
I HAVE TO CALL SIFU.
MOM, PLEASE POUR THE TEA WHILE I ANSWER THE PHONE.
RING RING
JOY, SLOW DOWN. I CAN'T UNDER-STAND YOU.

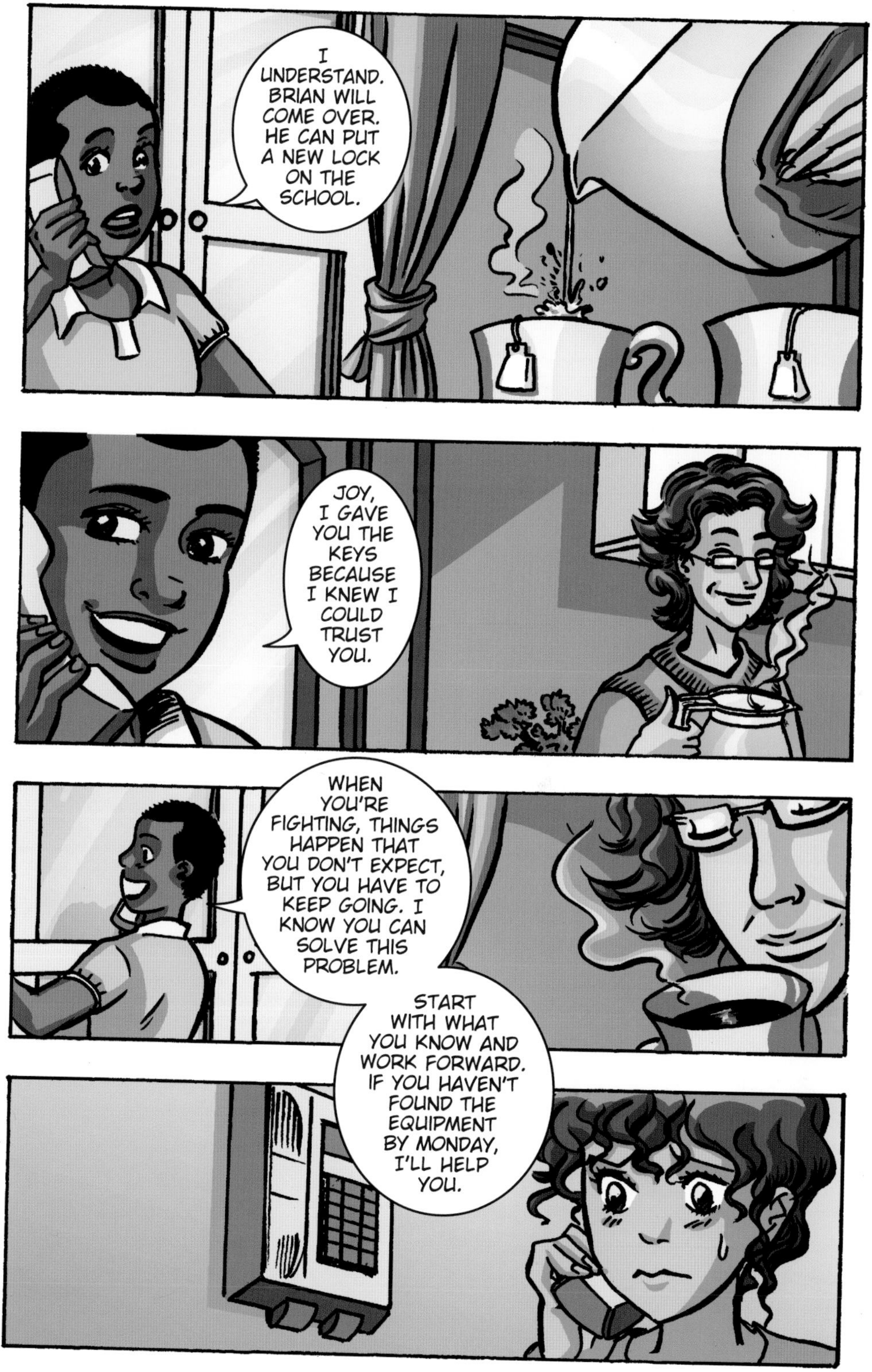
I UNDERSTAND. BRIAN WILL COME OVER. HE CAN PUT A NEW LOCK ON THE SCHOOL.
JOY, I GAVE YOU THE KEYS BECAUSE I KNEW I COULD TRUST YOU.
WHEN YOU'RE FIGHTING, THINGS HAPPEN THAT YOU DON'T EXPECT, BUT YOU HAVE TO KEEP GOING. I KNOW YOU CAN SOLVE THIS PROBLEM.
START WITH WHAT YOU KNOW AND WORK FORWARD. IF YOU HAVEN'T FOUND THE EQUIPMENT BY MONDAY, I'LL HELP YOU.

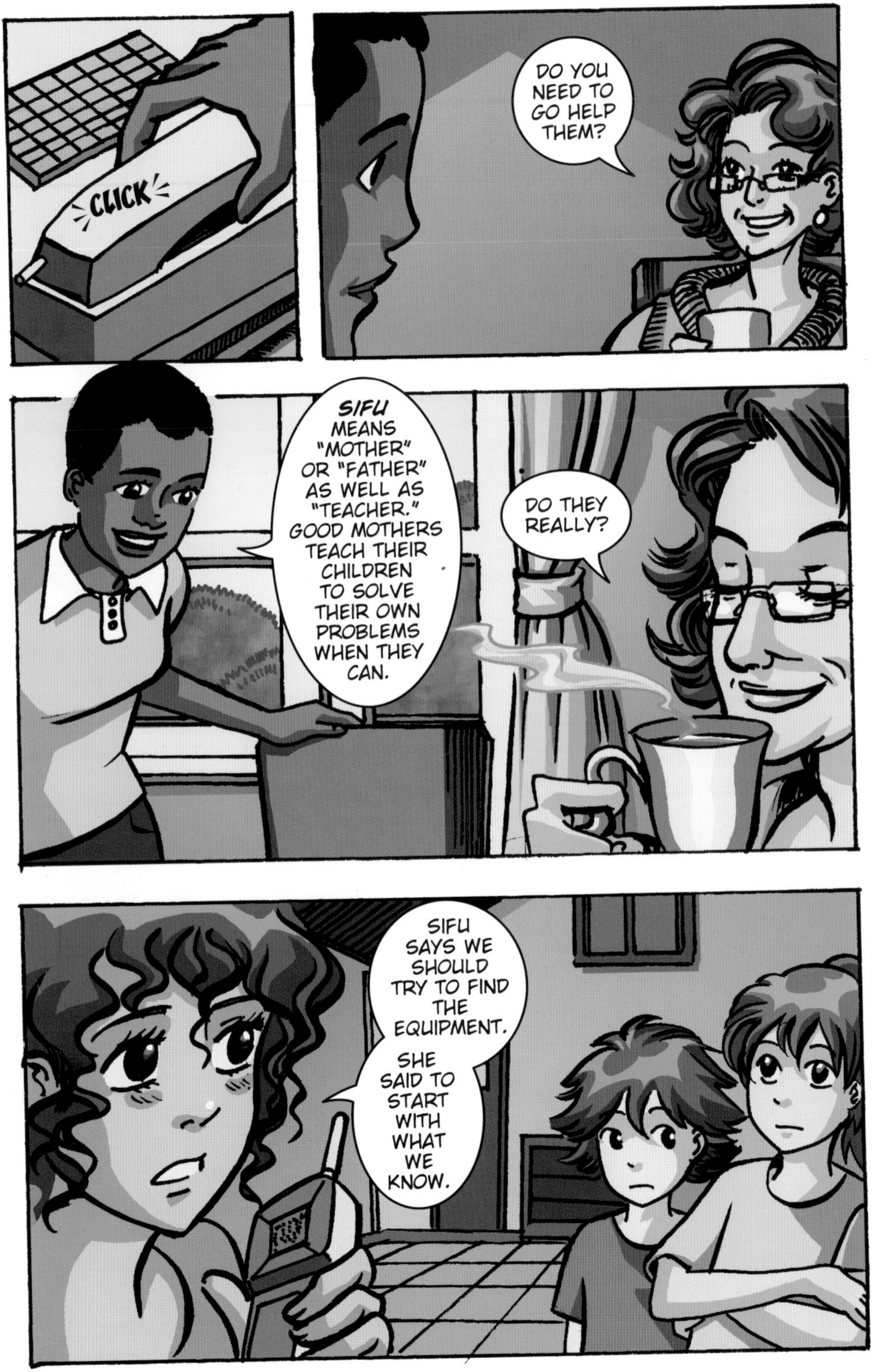
CLICK
DO YOU NEED TO GO HELP THEM?
SIFU MEANS "MOTHER" OR "FATHER" AS WELL AS "TEACHER." GOOD MOTHERS TEACH THEIR CHILDREN TO SOLVE THEIR OWN PROBLEMS WHEN THEY CAN.
DO THEY REALLY?
SIFU SAYS WE SHOULD TRY TO FIND THE EQUIPMENT.
SHE SAID TO START WITH WHAT WE KNOW.

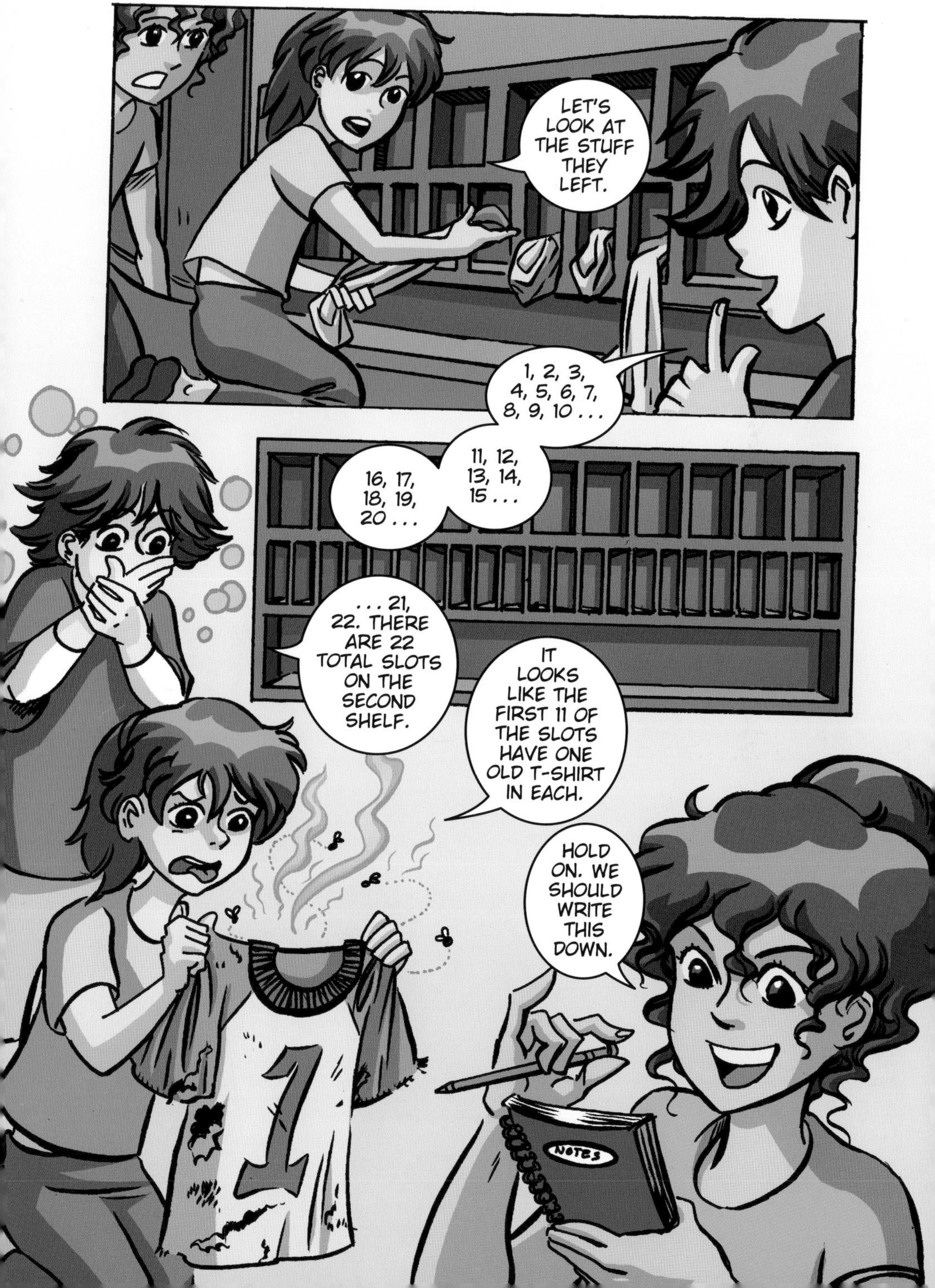
LET'S LOOK AT THE STUFF THEY LEFT.
1, 2, 3, 4, 5, 6, 7, 8, 9, 10 . . .
11, 12, 13, 14, 15 . . .
16, 17, 18, 19, 20 . . .
. . . 21, 22. THERE ARE 22 TOTAL SLOTS ON THE SECOND SHELF.
IT LOOKS LIKE THE FIRST 11 OF THE SLOTS HAVE ONE OLD T-SHIRT IN EACH.
HOLD ON. WE SHOULD WRITE THIS DOWN.
NOTES

Top shelf

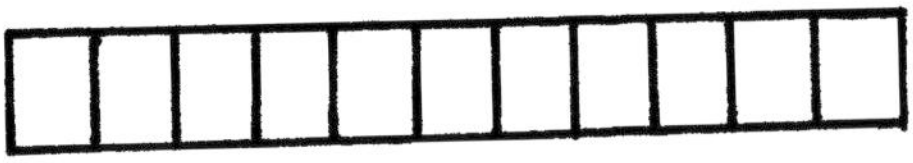

Middle shelf
22 total slots.
11 slots have one T-shirt in each. The rest have one pair of shorts in each.

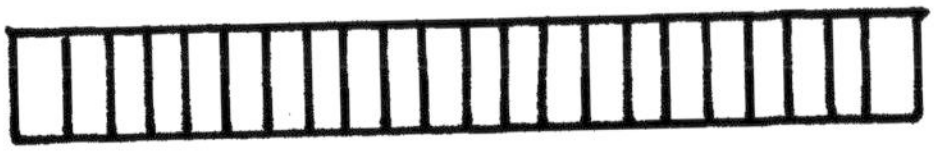

Bottom shelf
1 soccer ball.

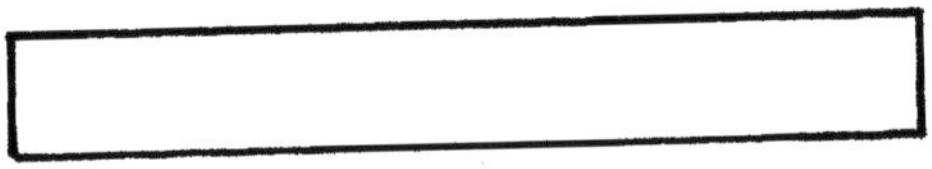

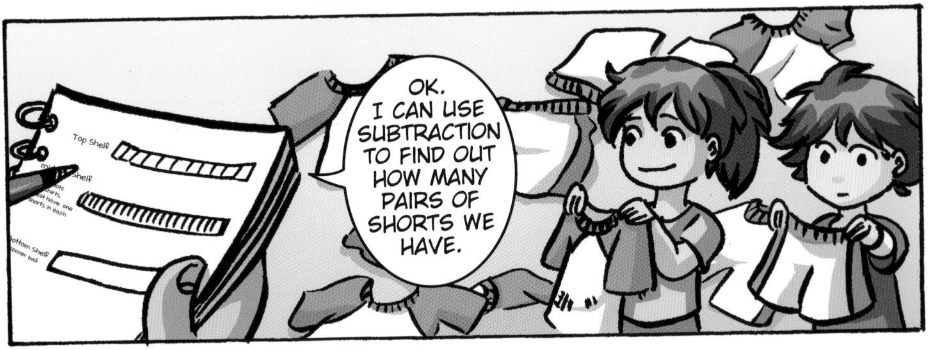
OK. I CAN USE SUBTRACTION TO FIND OUT HOW MANY PAIRS OF SHORTS WE HAVE.

Middle shelf
22 total slots.
11 slots have one T-shirt in each. The rest have one pair of shorts in each.
22 − 11 = 11 slots have shorts.

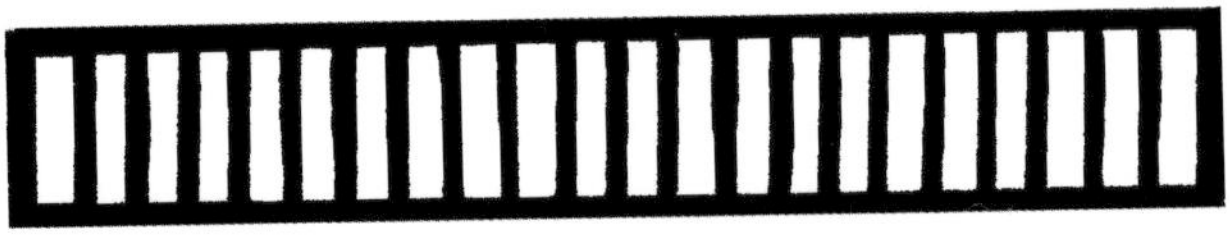

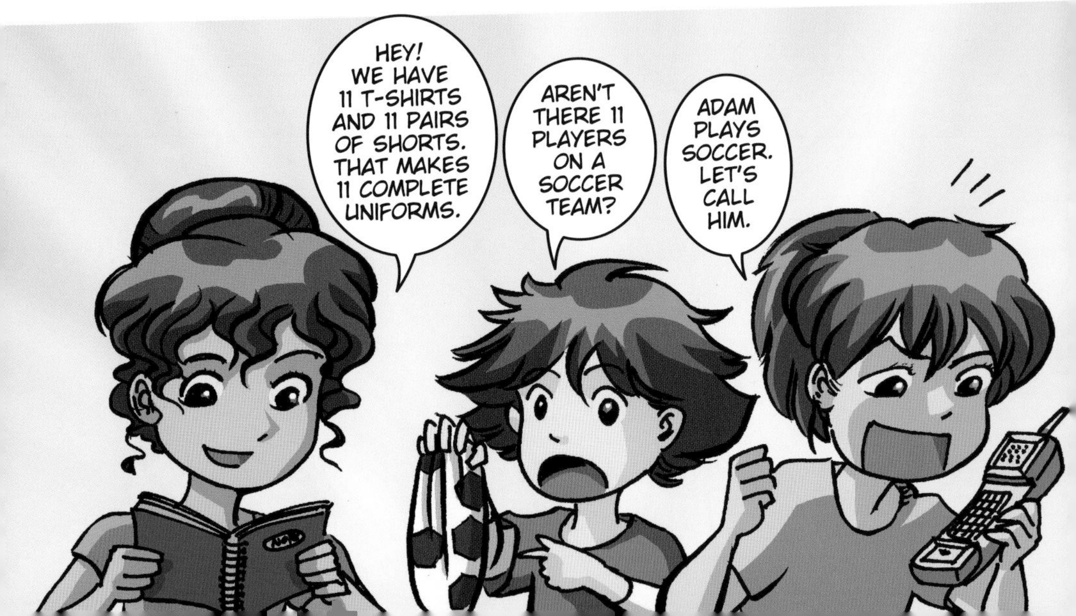
HEY! WE HAVE 11 T-SHIRTS AND 11 PAIRS OF SHORTS. THAT MAKES 11 COMPLETE UNIFORMS.
AREN'T THERE 11 PLAYERS ON A SOCCER TEAM?
ADAM PLAYS SOCCER. LET'S CALL HIM.

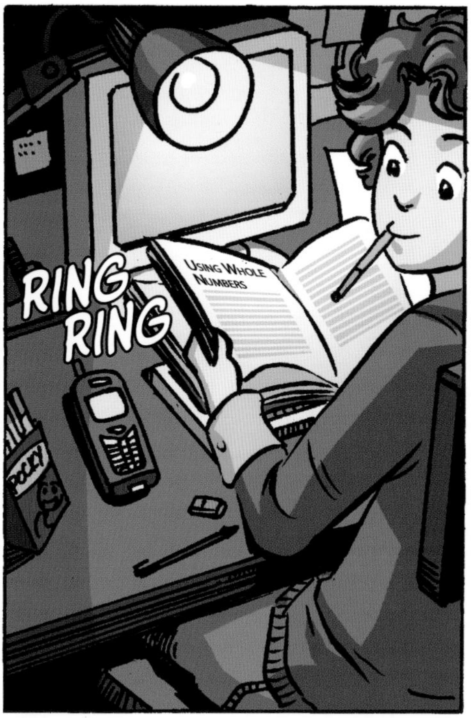
RING RING
USING WHOLE NUMBERS
POCKY

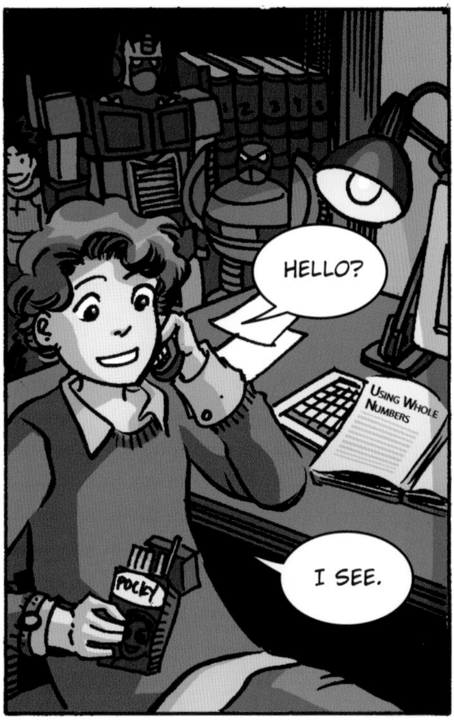
HELLO?
USING WHOLE NUMBERS
I SEE.
POCKY

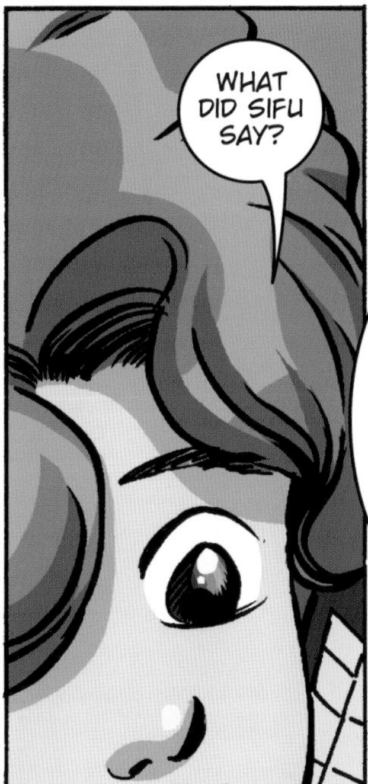
WHAT DID SIFU SAY?

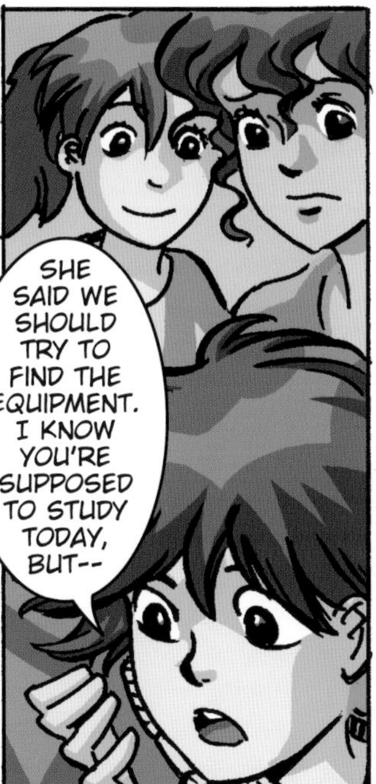
SHE SAID WE SHOULD TRY TO FIND THE EQUIPMENT. I KNOW YOU'RE SUPPOSED TO STUDY TODAY, BUT--

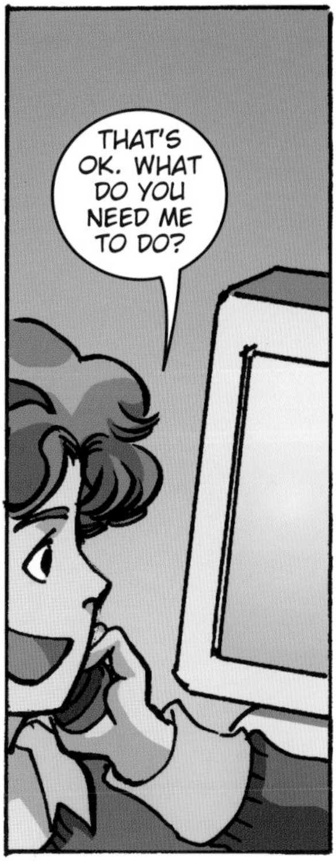
THAT'S OK. WHAT DO YOU NEED ME TO DO?

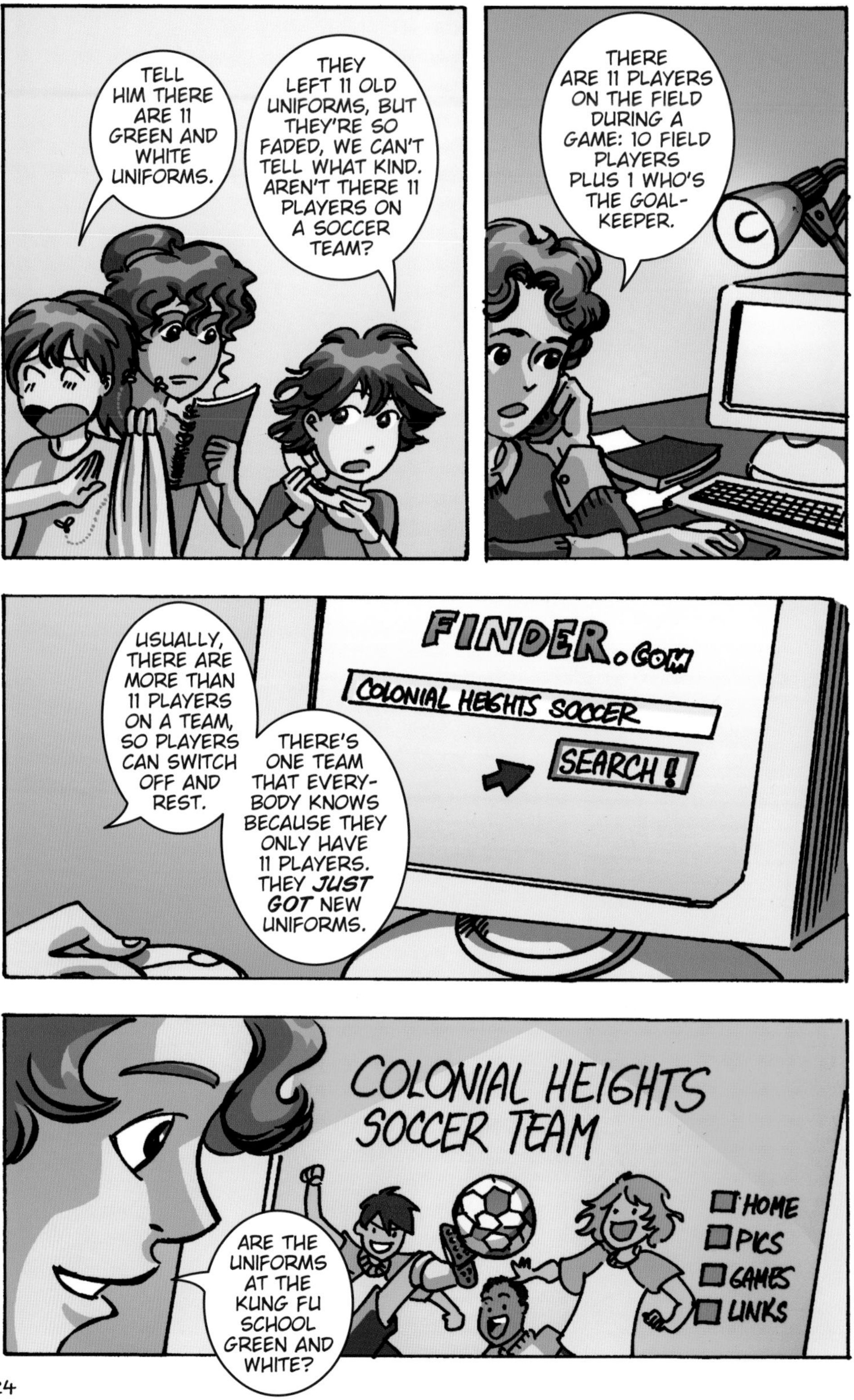
TELL HIM THERE ARE 11 GREEN AND WHITE UNIFORMS.
THEY LEFT 11 OLD UNIFORMS, BUT THEY'RE SO FADED, WE CAN'T TELL WHAT KIND. AREN'T THERE 11 PLAYERS ON A SOCCER TEAM?
THERE ARE 11 PLAYERS ON THE FIELD DURING A GAME: 10 FIELD PLAYERS PLUS 1 WHO'S THE GOAL-KEEPER.
USUALLY, THERE ARE MORE THAN 11 PLAYERS ON A TEAM, SO PLAYERS CAN SWITCH OFF AND REST.
FINDER.COM
COLONIAL HEIGHTS SOCCER
SEARCH!
THERE'S ONE TEAM THAT EVERY-BODY KNOWS BECAUSE THEY ONLY HAVE 11 PLAYERS. THEY *JUST GOT* NEW UNIFORMS.
COLONIAL HEIGHTS SOCCER TEAM
HOME
PICS
GAMES
LINKS
ARE THE UNIFORMS AT THE KUNG FU SCHOOL GREEN AND WHITE?

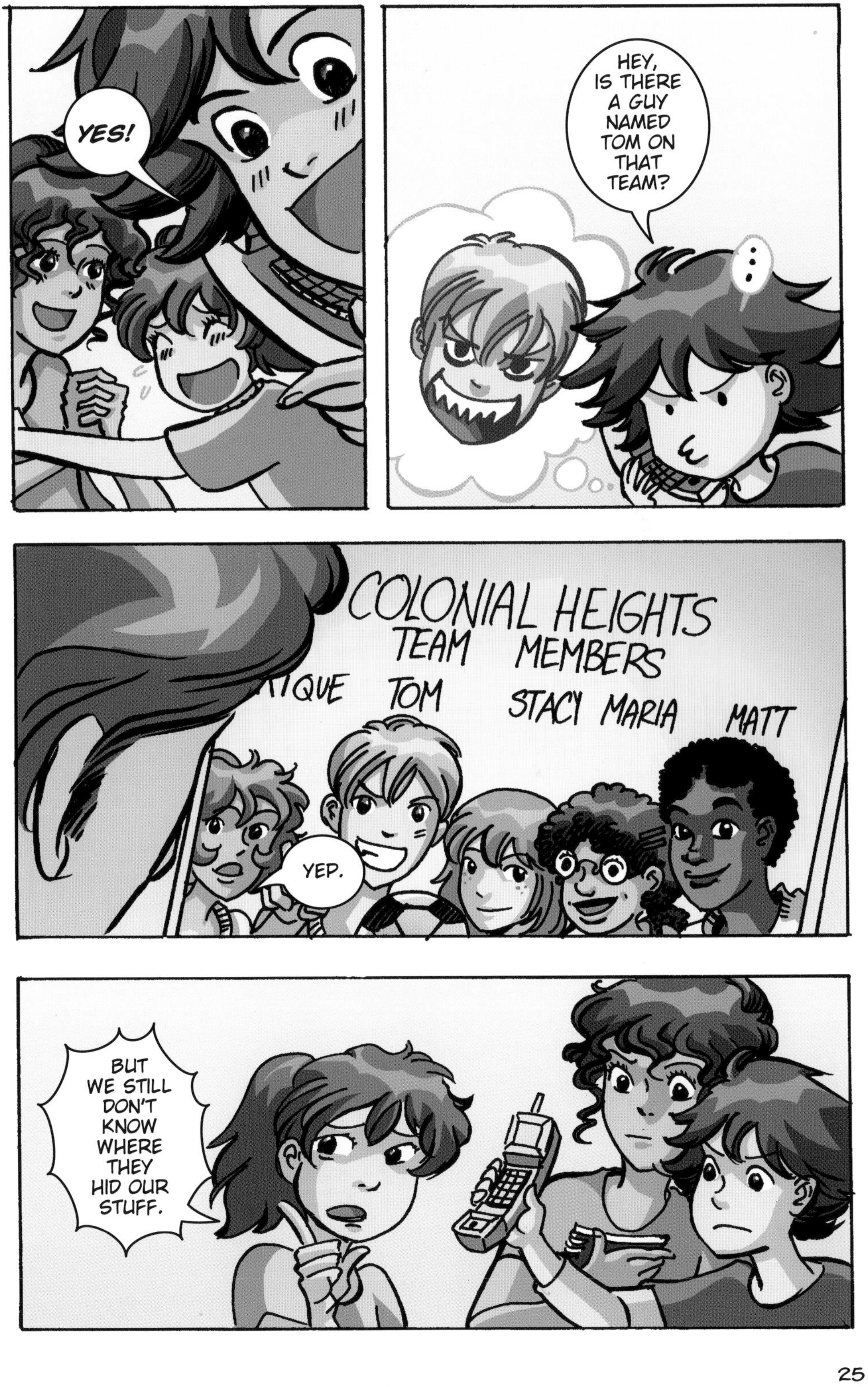
YES!
HEY, IS THERE A GUY NAMED TOM ON THAT TEAM?
...
COLONIAL HEIGHTS TEAM MEMBERS
TOM STACY MARIA MATT
YEP.
BUT WE STILL DON'T KNOW WHERE THEY HID OUR STUFF.

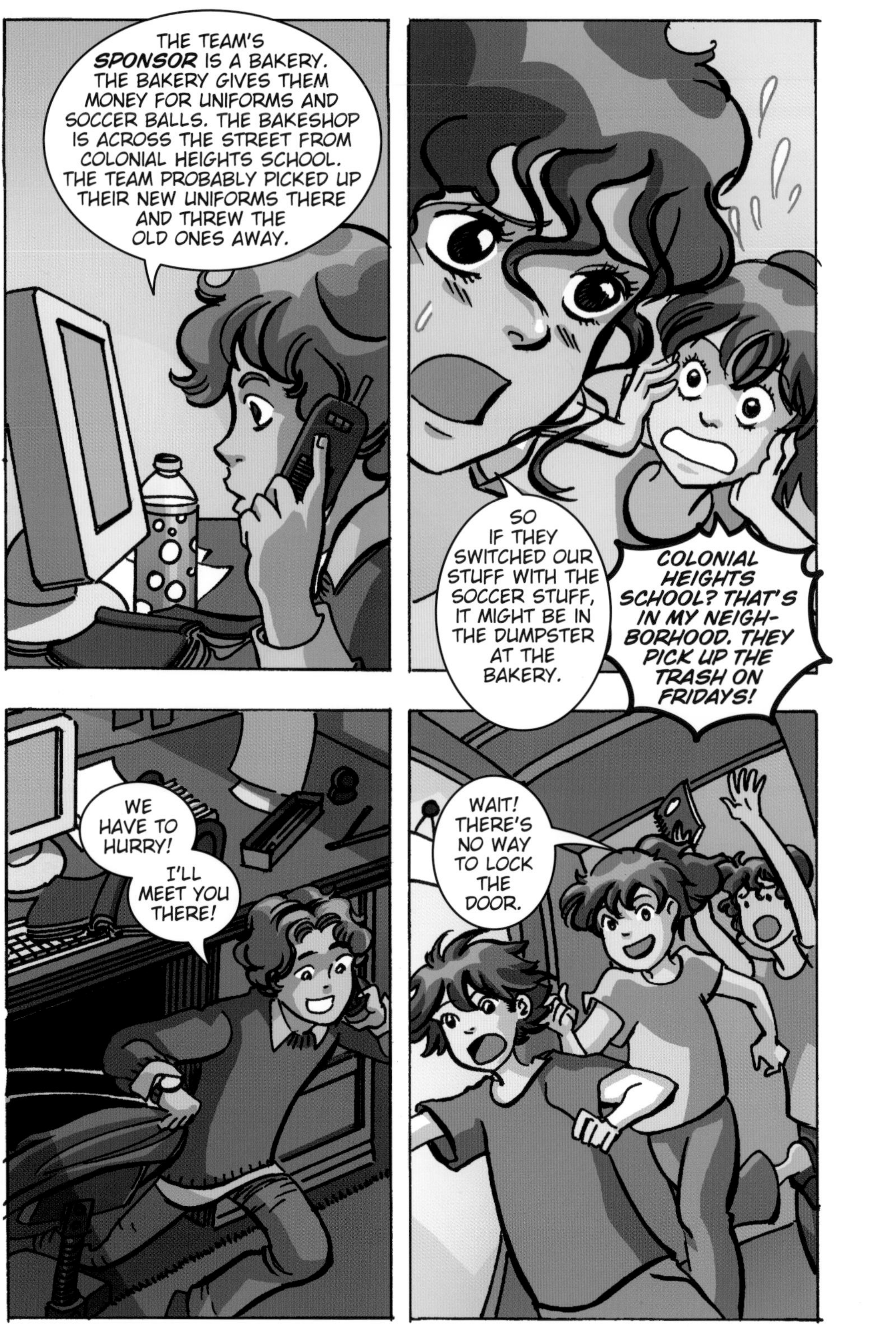
THE TEAM'S **SPONSOR** IS A BAKERY. THE BAKERY GIVES THEM MONEY FOR UNIFORMS AND SOCCER BALLS. THE BAKESHOP IS ACROSS THE STREET FROM COLONIAL HEIGHTS SCHOOL. THE TEAM PROBABLY PICKED UP THEIR NEW UNIFORMS THERE AND THREW THE OLD ONES AWAY.
SO IF THEY SWITCHED OUR STUFF WITH THE SOCCER STUFF, IT MIGHT BE IN THE DUMPSTER AT THE BAKERY.
COLONIAL HEIGHTS SCHOOL? THAT'S IN MY NEIGHBORHOOD. THEY PICK UP THE TRASH ON FRIDAYS!
WE HAVE TO HURRY!
I'LL MEET YOU THERE!
WAIT! THERE'S NO WAY TO LOCK THE DOOR.

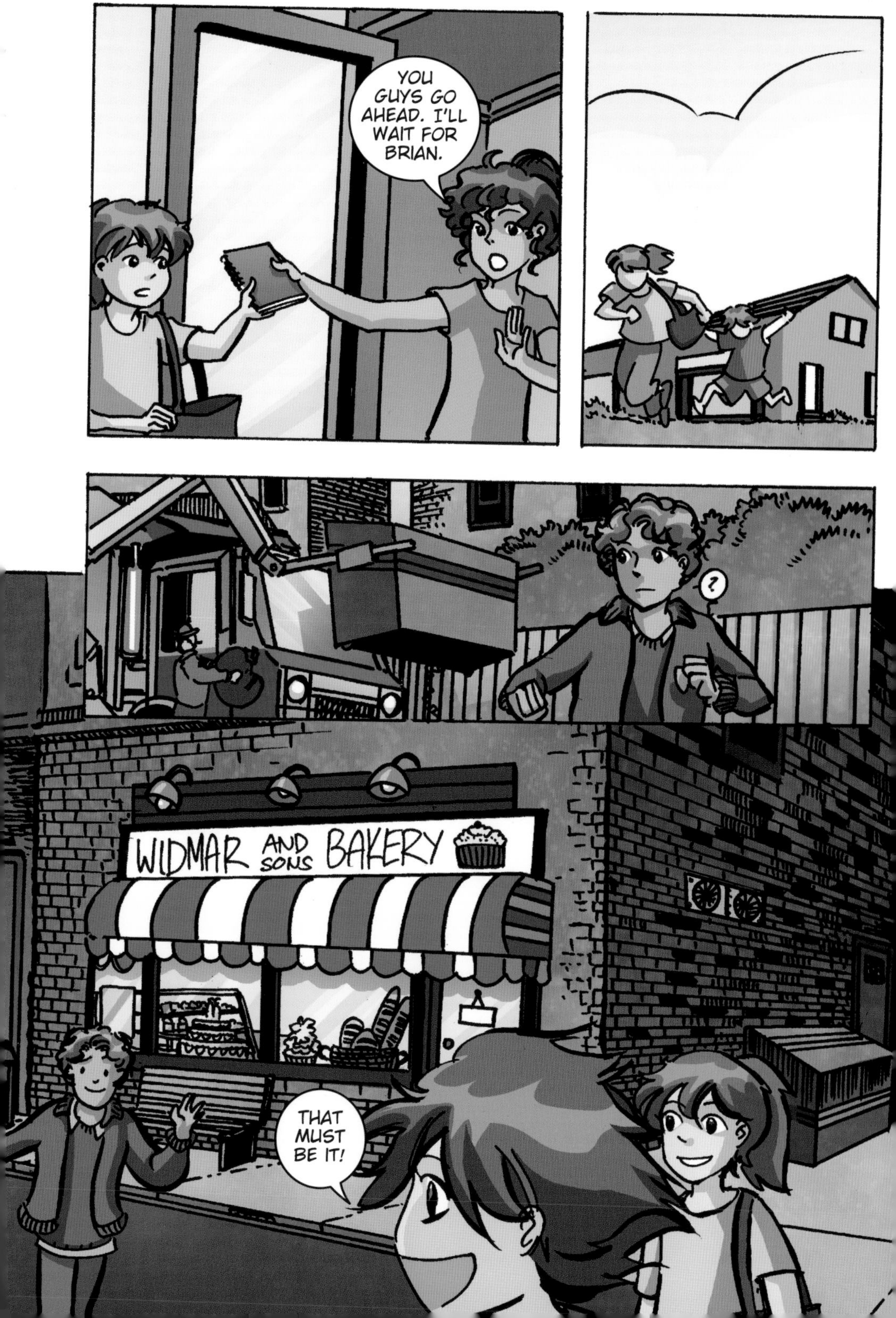
YOU GUYS GO AHEAD. I'LL WAIT FOR BRIAN.
?
WIDMAR AND SONS BAKERY
THAT MUST BE IT!

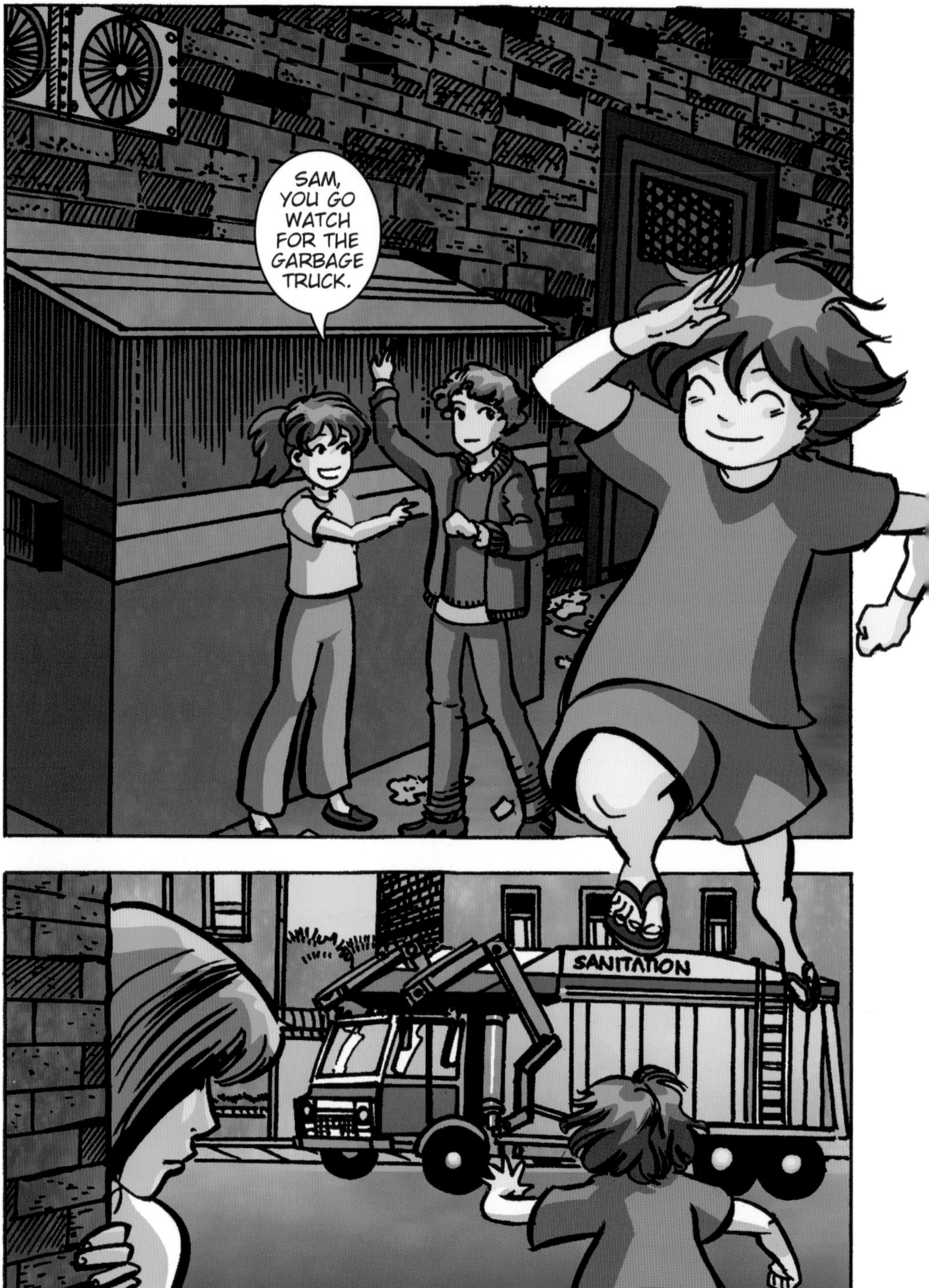
SAM, YOU GO WATCH FOR THE GARBAGE TRUCK.
SANITATION

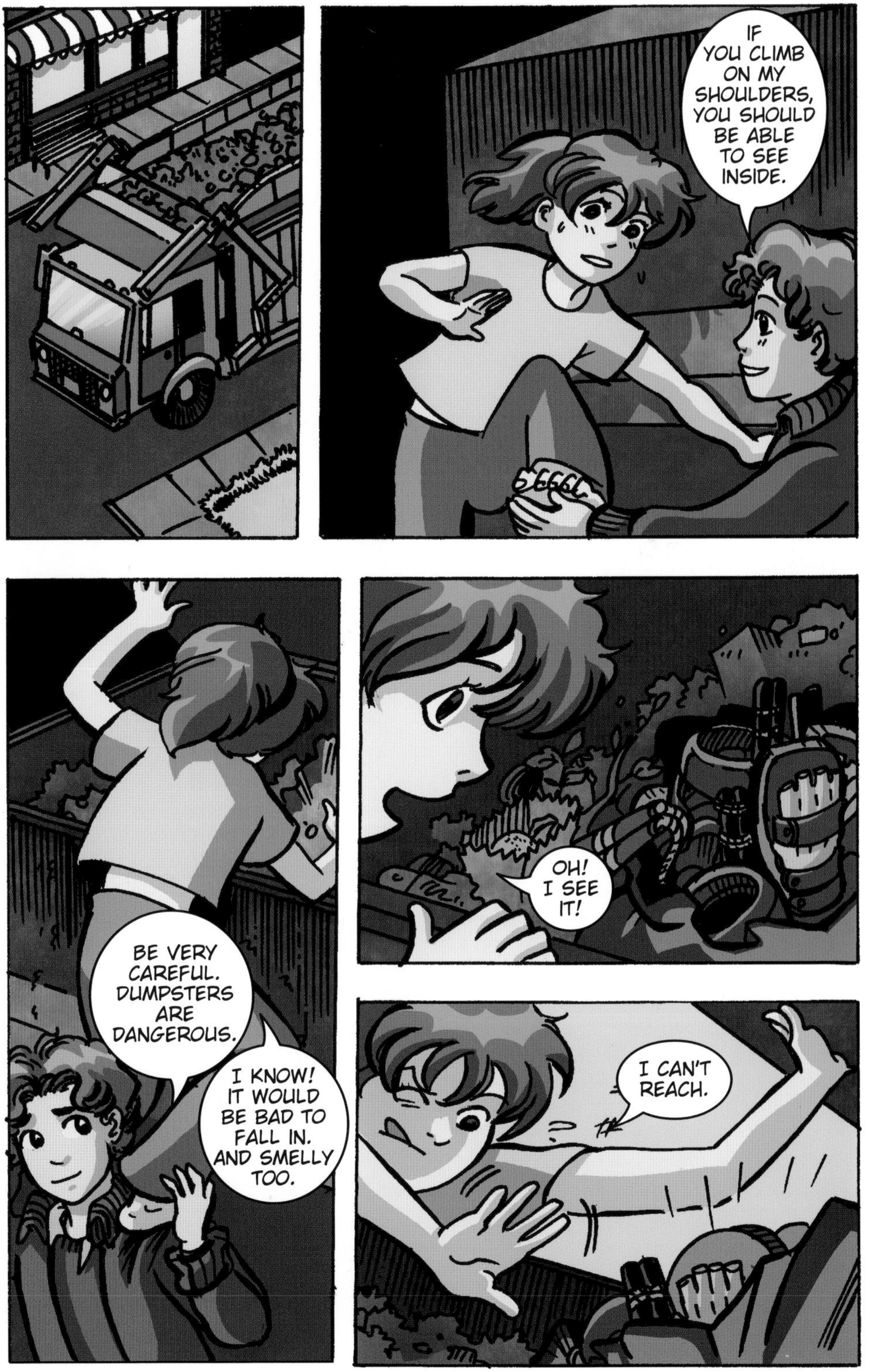
IF YOU CLIMB ON MY SHOULDERS, YOU SHOULD BE ABLE TO SEE INSIDE.
BE VERY CAREFUL. DUMPSTERS ARE DANGEROUS.
I KNOW! IT WOULD BE BAD TO FALL IN. AND SMELLY TOO.
OH! I SEE IT!
I CAN'T REACH.

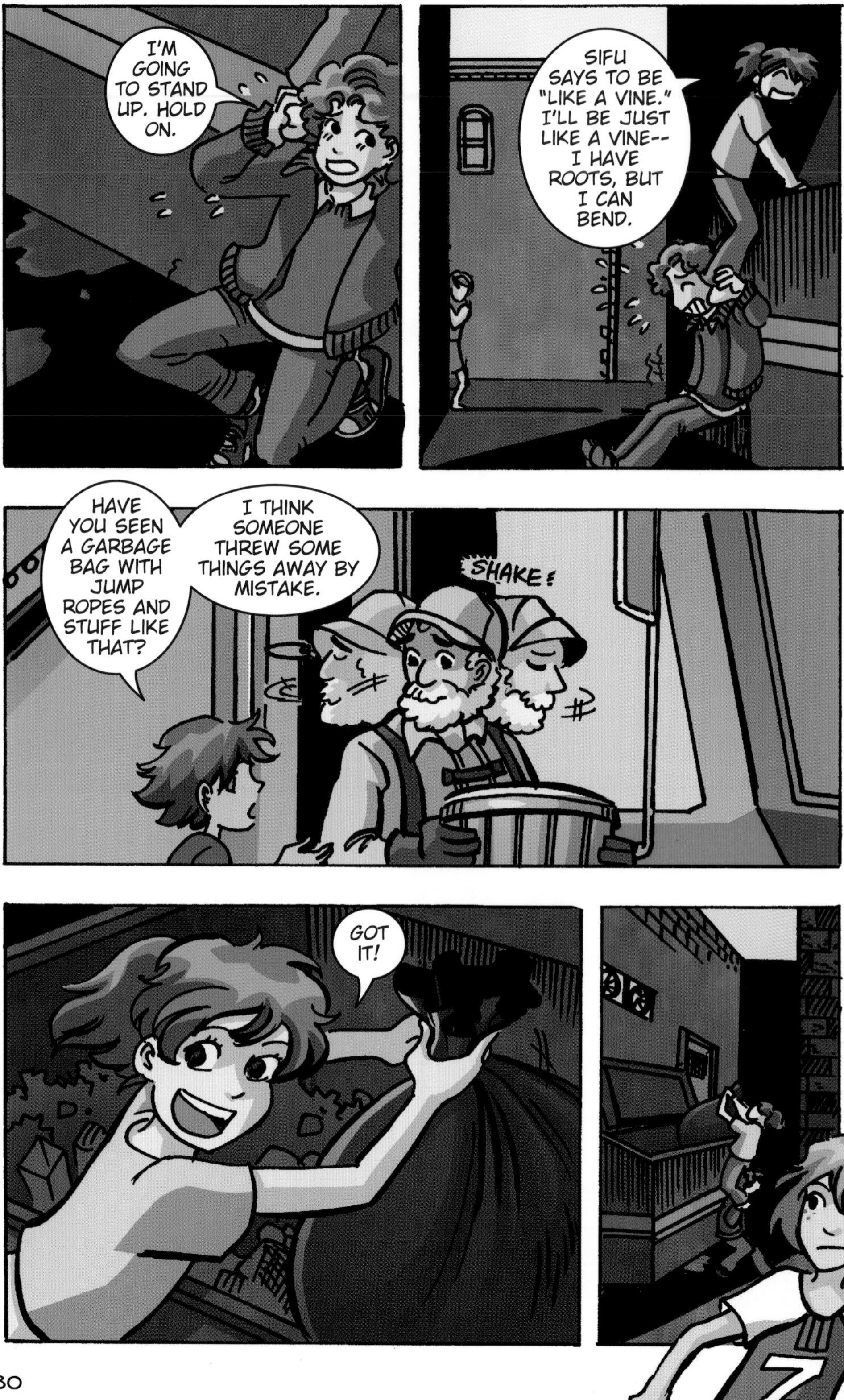
I'M GOING TO STAND UP. HOLD ON.
SIFU SAYS TO BE "LIKE A VINE." I'LL BE JUST LIKE A VINE-- I HAVE ROOTS, BUT I CAN BEND.
HAVE YOU SEEN A GARBAGE BAG WITH JUMP ROPES AND STUFF LIKE THAT?
I THINK SOMEONE THREW SOME THINGS AWAY BY MISTAKE.
SHAKE
GOT IT!

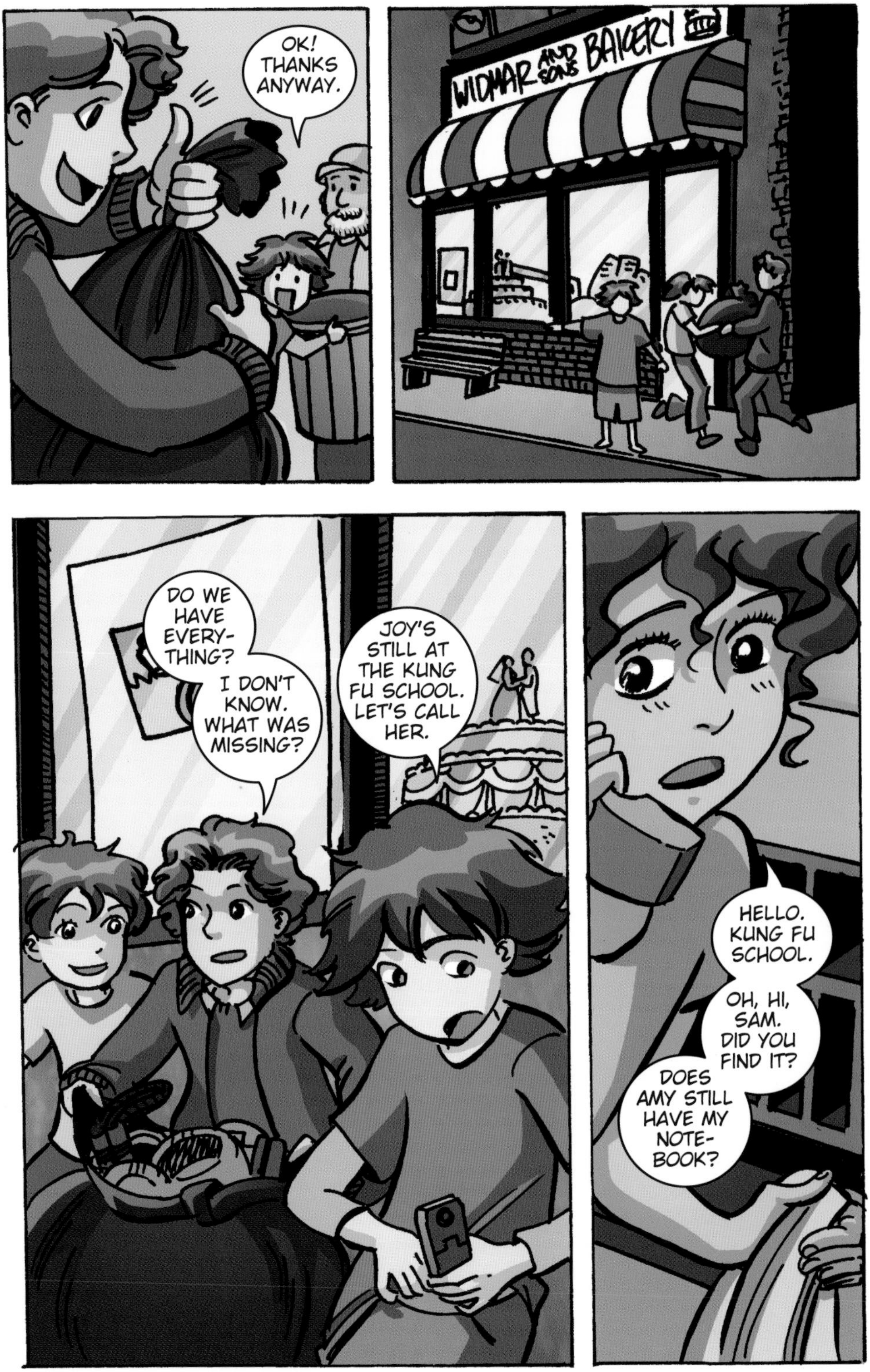
OK! THANKS ANYWAY.
WIDMAR AND SONS BAKERY
DO WE HAVE EVERY-THING?
I DON'T KNOW. WHAT WAS MISSING?
JOY'S STILL AT THE KUNG FU SCHOOL. LET'S CALL HER.
HELLO. KUNG FU SCHOOL.
OH, HI, SAM. DID YOU FIND IT?
DOES AMY STILL HAVE MY NOTE-BOOK?

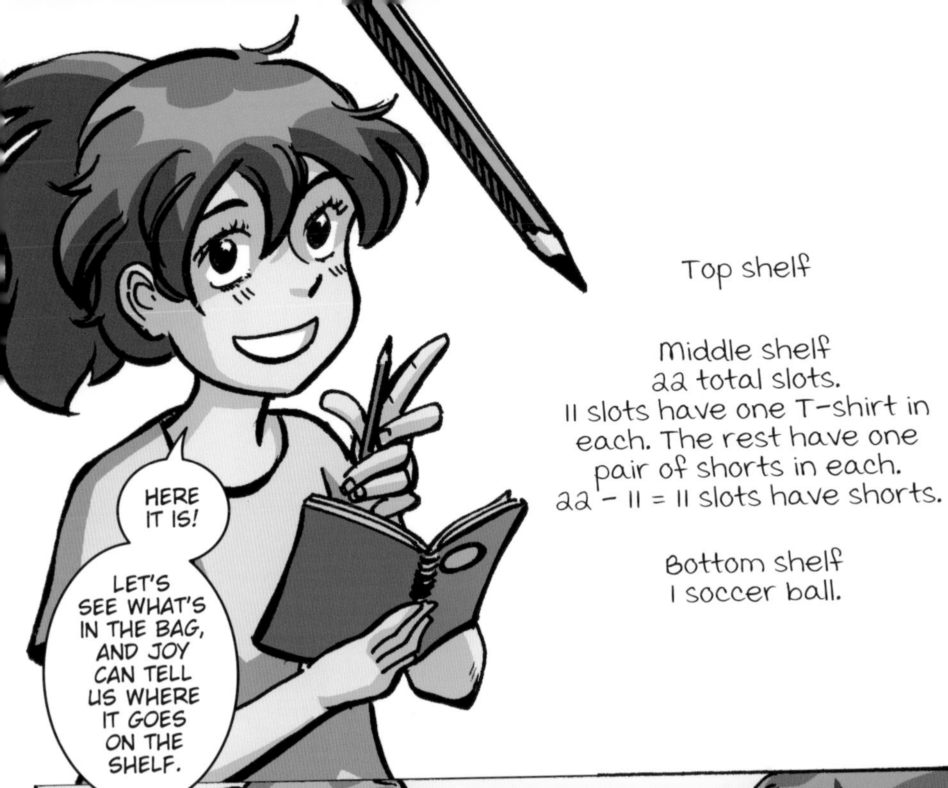
Top shelf
Middle shelf
22 total slots.
11 slots have one T-shirt in each. The rest have one pair of shorts in each.
22 - 11 = 11 slots have shorts.
Bottom shelf
1 soccer ball.
HERE IT IS!
LET'S SEE WHAT'S IN THE BAG, AND JOY CAN TELL US WHERE IT GOES ON THE SHELF.

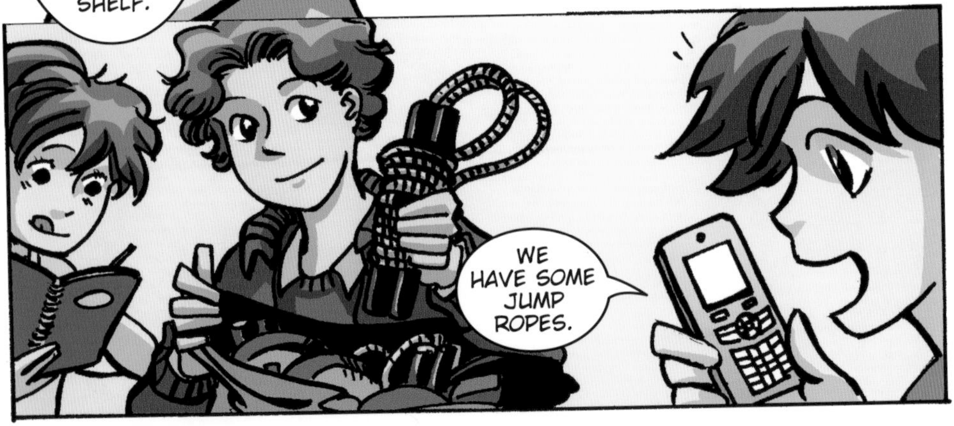
WE HAVE SOME JUMP ROPES.

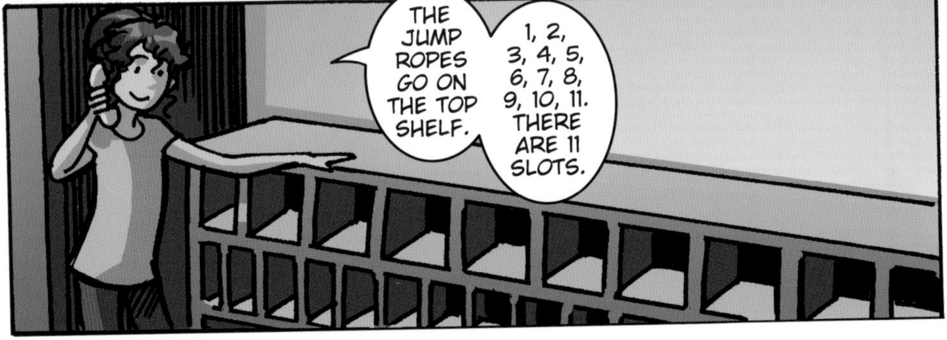
THE JUMP ROPES GO ON THE TOP SHELF.
1, 2, 3, 4, 5, 6, 7, 8, 9, 10, 11. THERE ARE 11 SLOTS.

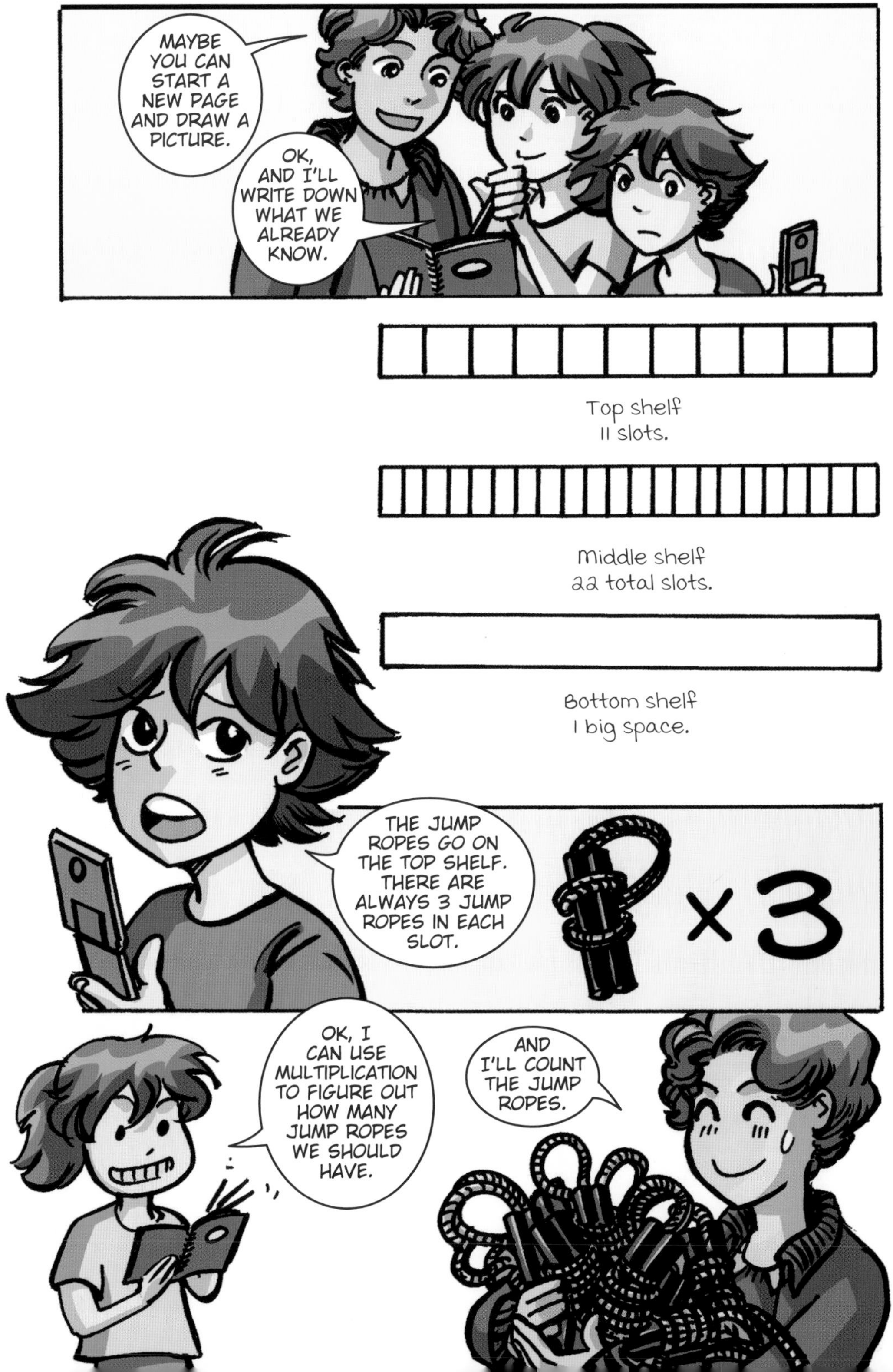
MAYBE YOU CAN START A NEW PAGE AND DRAW A PICTURE.
OK, AND I'LL WRITE DOWN WHAT WE ALREADY KNOW.
Top shelf
11 slots.
Middle shelf
22 total slots.
Bottom shelf
1 big space.
THE JUMP ROPES GO ON THE TOP SHELF. THERE ARE ALWAYS 3 JUMP ROPES IN EACH SLOT.
×3
OK, I CAN USE MULTIPLICATION TO FIGURE OUT HOW MANY JUMP ROPES WE SHOULD HAVE.
AND I'LL COUNT THE JUMP ROPES.

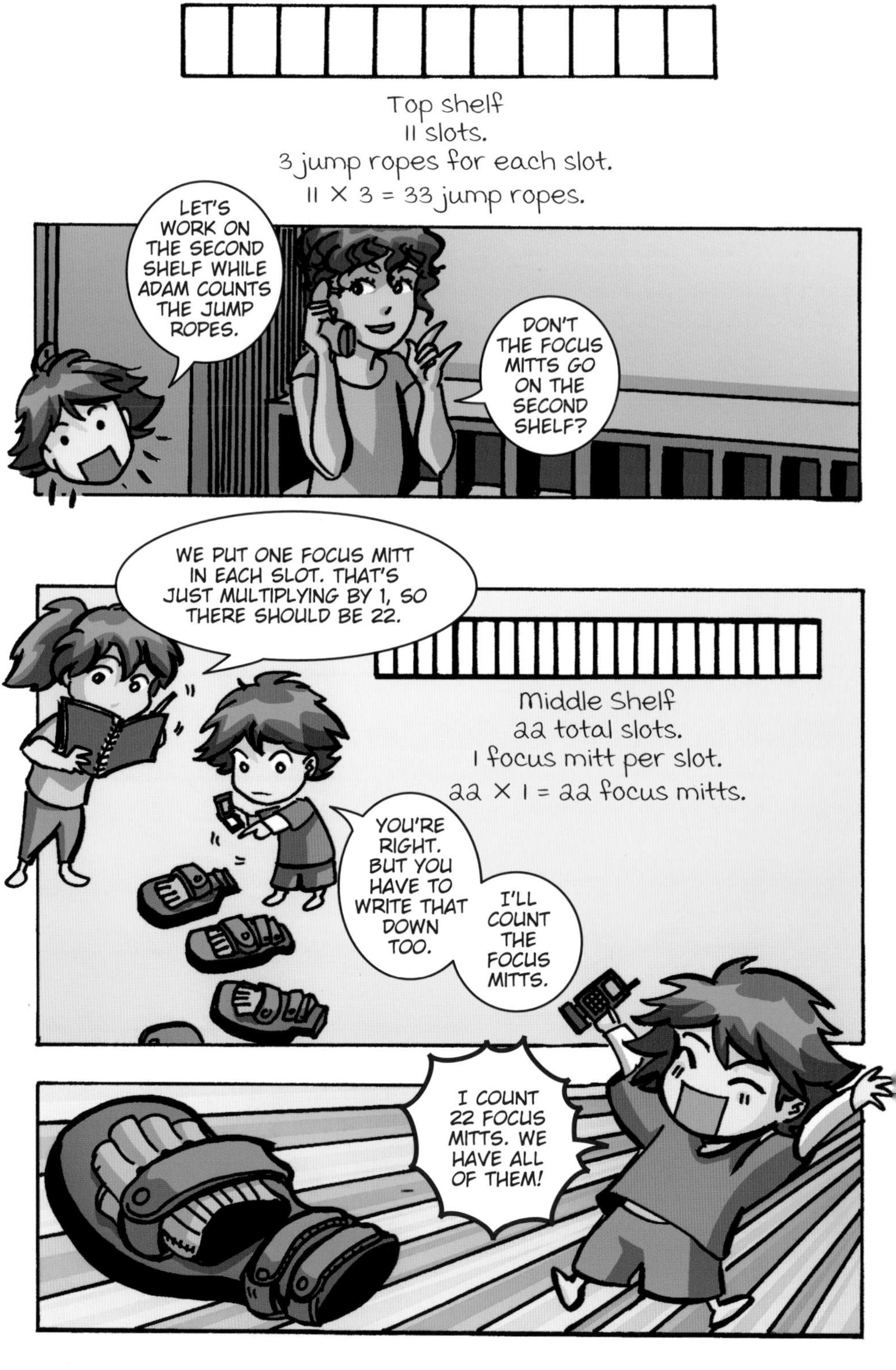
Top shelf
11 slots.
3 jump ropes for each slot.
11 × 3 = 33 jump ropes.
LET'S WORK ON THE SECOND SHELF WHILE ADAM COUNTS THE JUMP ROPES.
DON'T THE FOCUS MITTS GO ON THE SECOND SHELF?
WE PUT ONE FOCUS MITT IN EACH SLOT. THAT'S JUST MULTIPLYING BY 1, SO THERE SHOULD BE 22.
Middle Shelf
22 total slots.
1 focus mitt per slot.
22 × 1 = 22 focus mitts.
YOU'RE RIGHT. BUT YOU HAVE TO WRITE THAT DOWN TOO.
I'LL COUNT THE FOCUS MITTS.
I COUNT 22 FOCUS MITTS. WE HAVE ALL OF THEM!

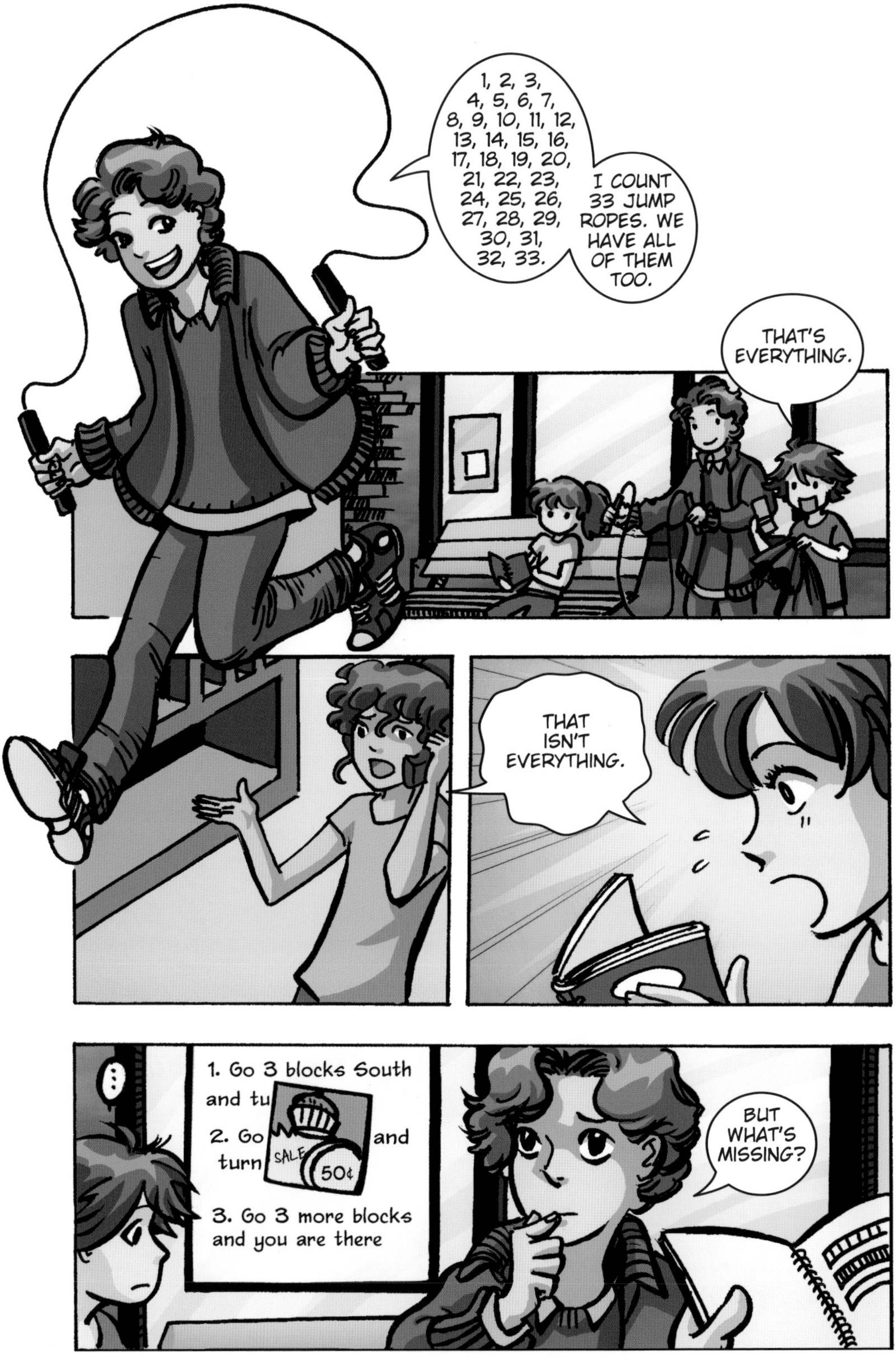
1, 2, 3, 4, 5, 6, 7, 8, 9, 10, 11, 12, 13, 14, 15, 16, 17, 18, 19, 20, 21, 22, 23, 24, 25, 26, 27, 28, 29, 30, 31, 32, 33.
I COUNT 33 JUMP ROPES. WE HAVE ALL OF THEM TOO.
THAT'S EVERYTHING.
THAT ISN'T EVERYTHING.
...
1. Go 3 blocks South and tu
2. Go and turn
SALE
50¢
3. Go 3 more blocks and you are there
BUT WHAT'S MISSING?

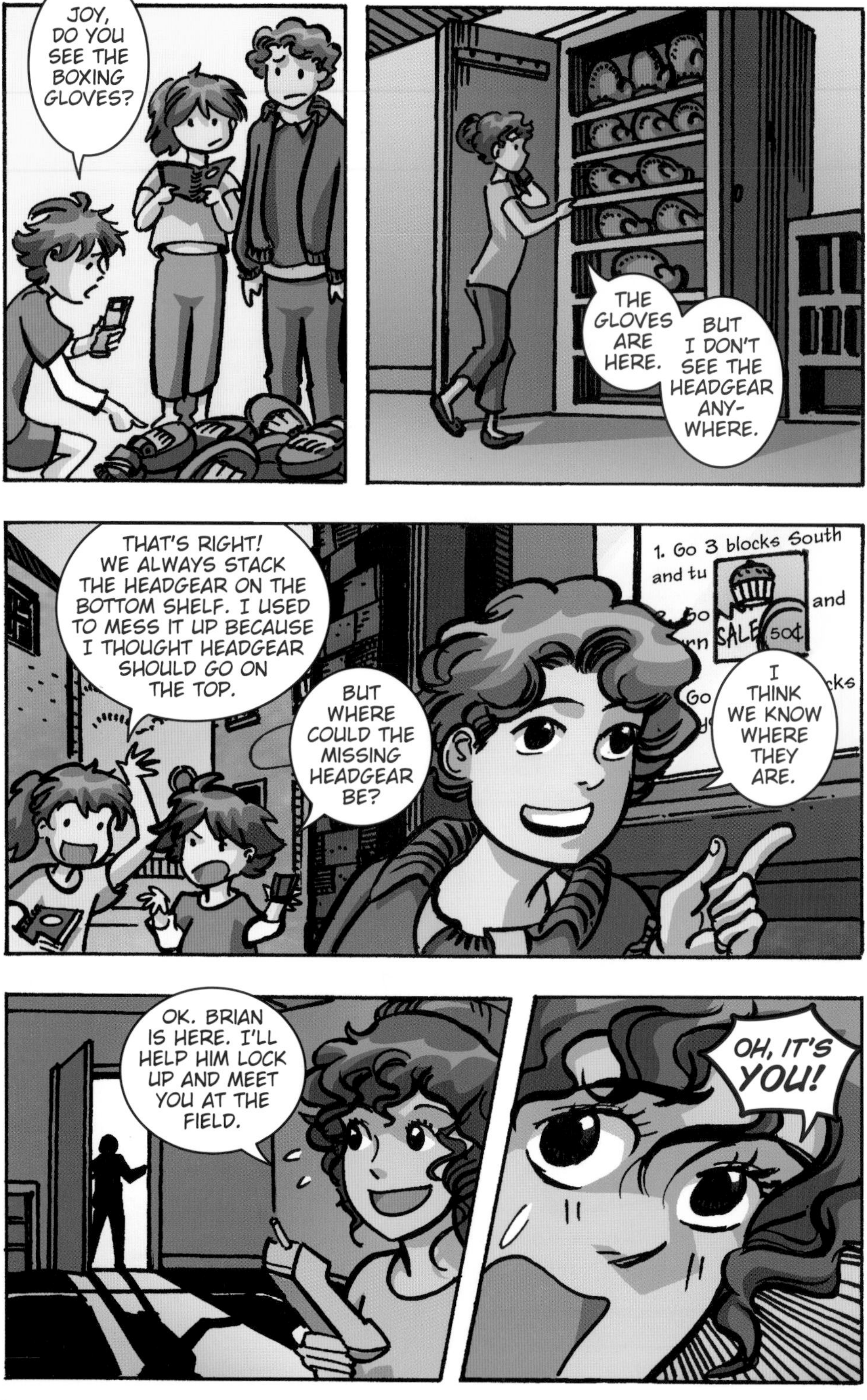
JOY, DO YOU SEE THE BOXING GLOVES?
THE GLOVES ARE HERE.
BUT I DON'T SEE THE HEADGEAR ANYWHERE.
THAT'S RIGHT! WE ALWAYS STACK THE HEADGEAR ON THE BOTTOM SHELF. I USED TO MESS IT UP BECAUSE I THOUGHT HEADGEAR SHOULD GO ON THE TOP.
BUT WHERE COULD THE MISSING HEADGEAR BE?
1. Go 3 blocks South and tu
SALE 50¢
I THINK WE KNOW WHERE THEY ARE.
OK. BRIAN IS HERE. I'LL HELP HIM LOCK UP AND MEET YOU AT THE FIELD.
OH, IT'S YOU!

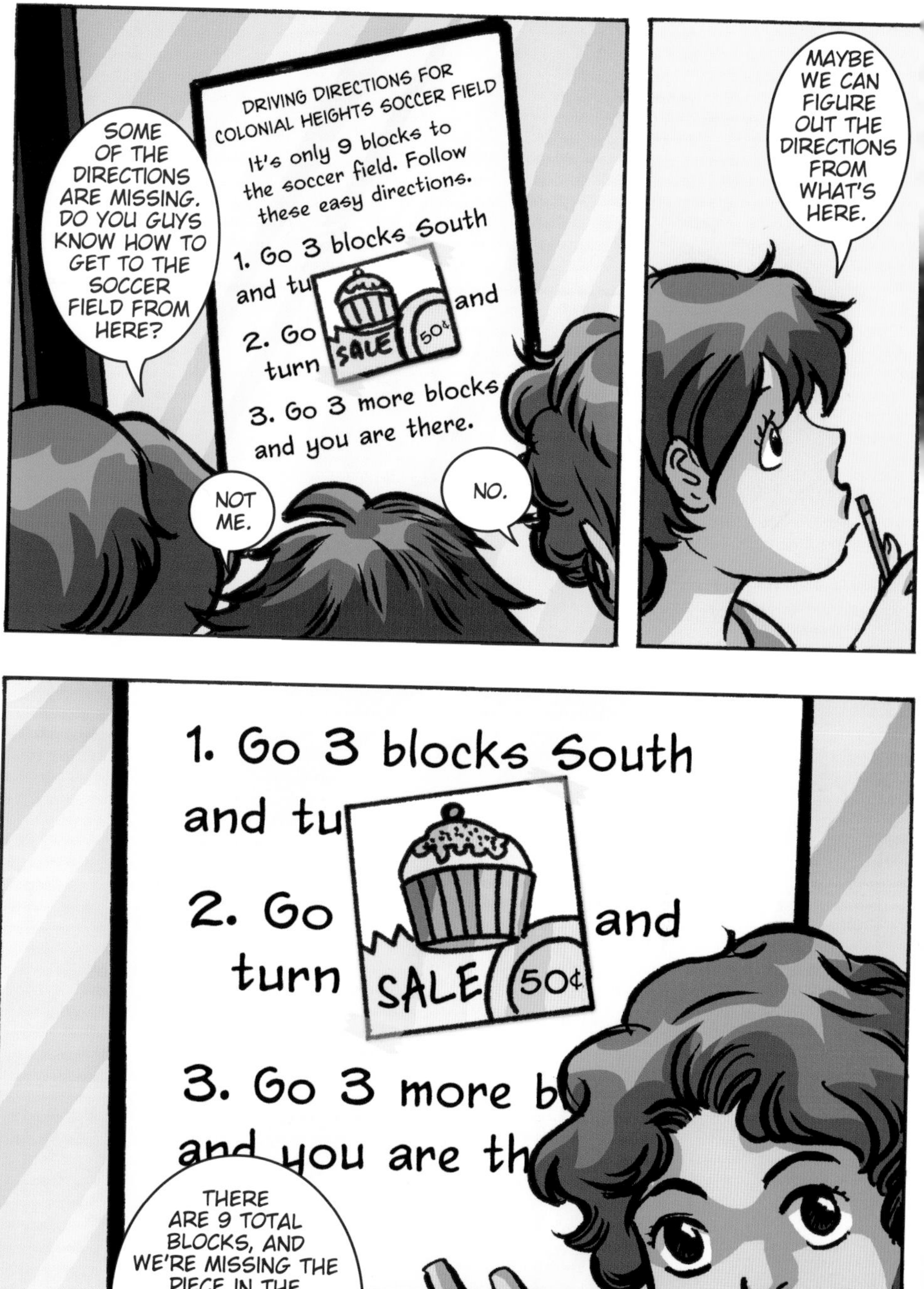
DRIVING DIRECTIONS FOR COLONIAL HEIGHTS SOCCER FIELD
It's only 9 blocks to the soccer field. Follow these easy directions.
1. Go 3 blocks South and tu
2. Go
and
turn
SALE
50¢
3. Go 3 more blocks and you are there.
SOME OF THE DIRECTIONS ARE MISSING. DO YOU GUYS KNOW HOW TO GET TO THE SOCCER FIELD FROM HERE?
NOT ME.
NO.
MAYBE WE CAN FIGURE OUT THE DIRECTIONS FROM WHAT'S HERE.
1. Go 3 blocks South
and tu
2. Go
and
turn
SALE
50¢
3. Go 3 more b
you are th
THERE ARE 9 TOTAL BLOCKS, AND WE'RE MISSING THE PIECE IN THE MIDDLE. SO LET'S BREAK THE TRIP INTO 3 EQUAL PIECES. WE SHOULD DIVIDE 9 BY 3.

9 total blocks divided into 3 equal parts.

Each part of the trip is $9 \div 3 = 3$ blocks long.

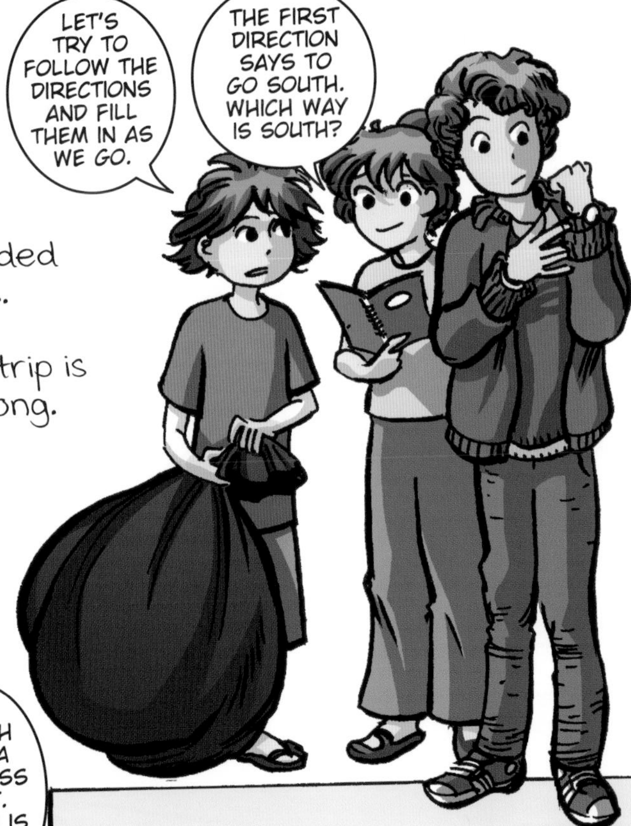
LET'S TRY TO FOLLOW THE DIRECTIONS AND FILL THEM IN AS WE GO.
THE FIRST DIRECTION SAYS TO GO SOUTH. WHICH WAY IS SOUTH?

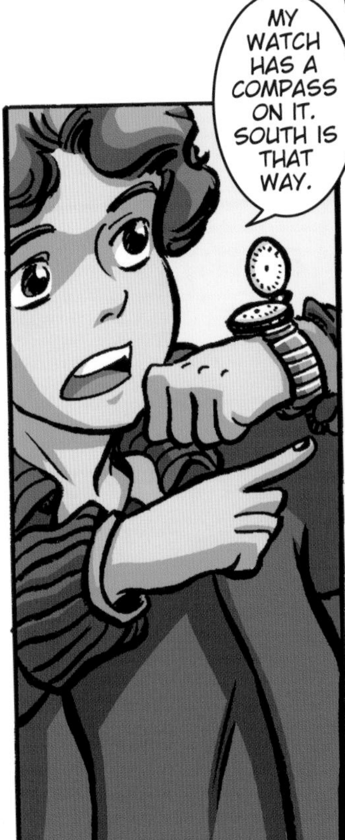
MY WATCH HAS A COMPASS ON IT. SOUTH IS THAT WAY.

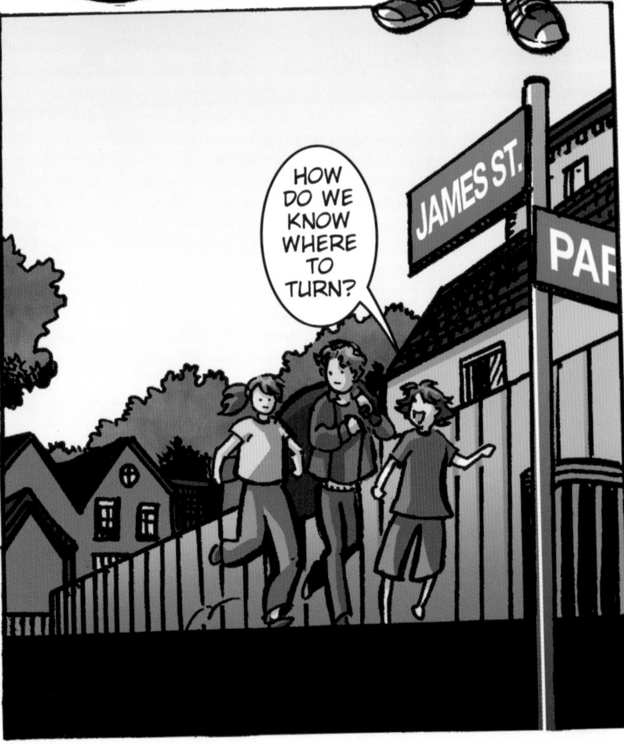
HOW DO WE KNOW WHERE TO TURN?
JAMES ST.

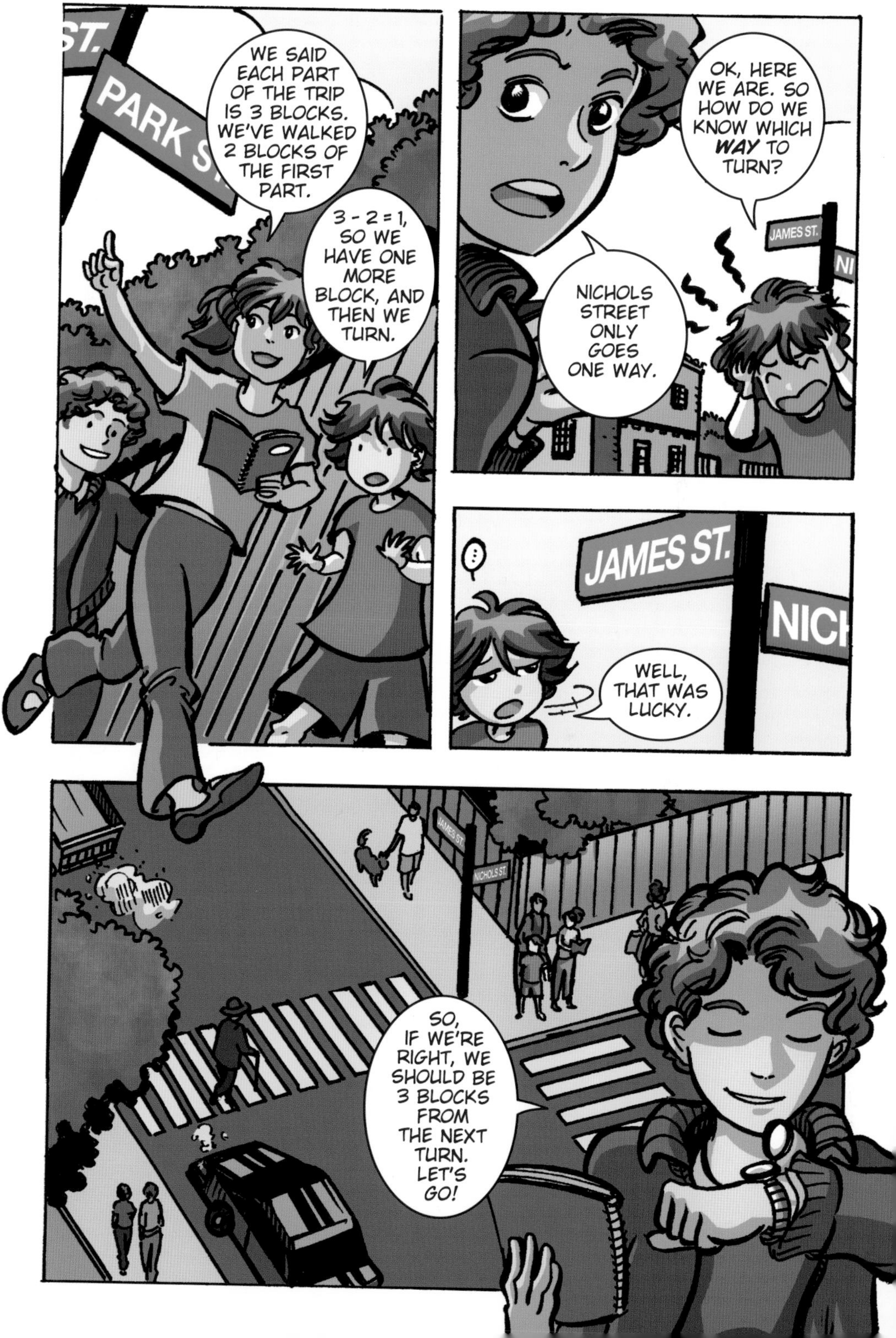
WE SAID EACH PART OF THE TRIP IS 3 BLOCKS. WE'VE WALKED 2 BLOCKS OF THE FIRST PART.
3 - 2 = 1, SO WE HAVE ONE MORE BLOCK, AND THEN WE TURN.
OK, HERE WE ARE. SO HOW DO WE KNOW WHICH ***WAY*** TO TURN?
JAMES ST.
NICHOLS STREET ONLY GOES ONE WAY.
JAMES ST.
WELL, THAT WAS LUCKY.
JAMES ST.
NICHOLS ST.
SO, IF WE'RE RIGHT, WE SHOULD BE 3 BLOCKS FROM THE NEXT TURN. LET'S GO!

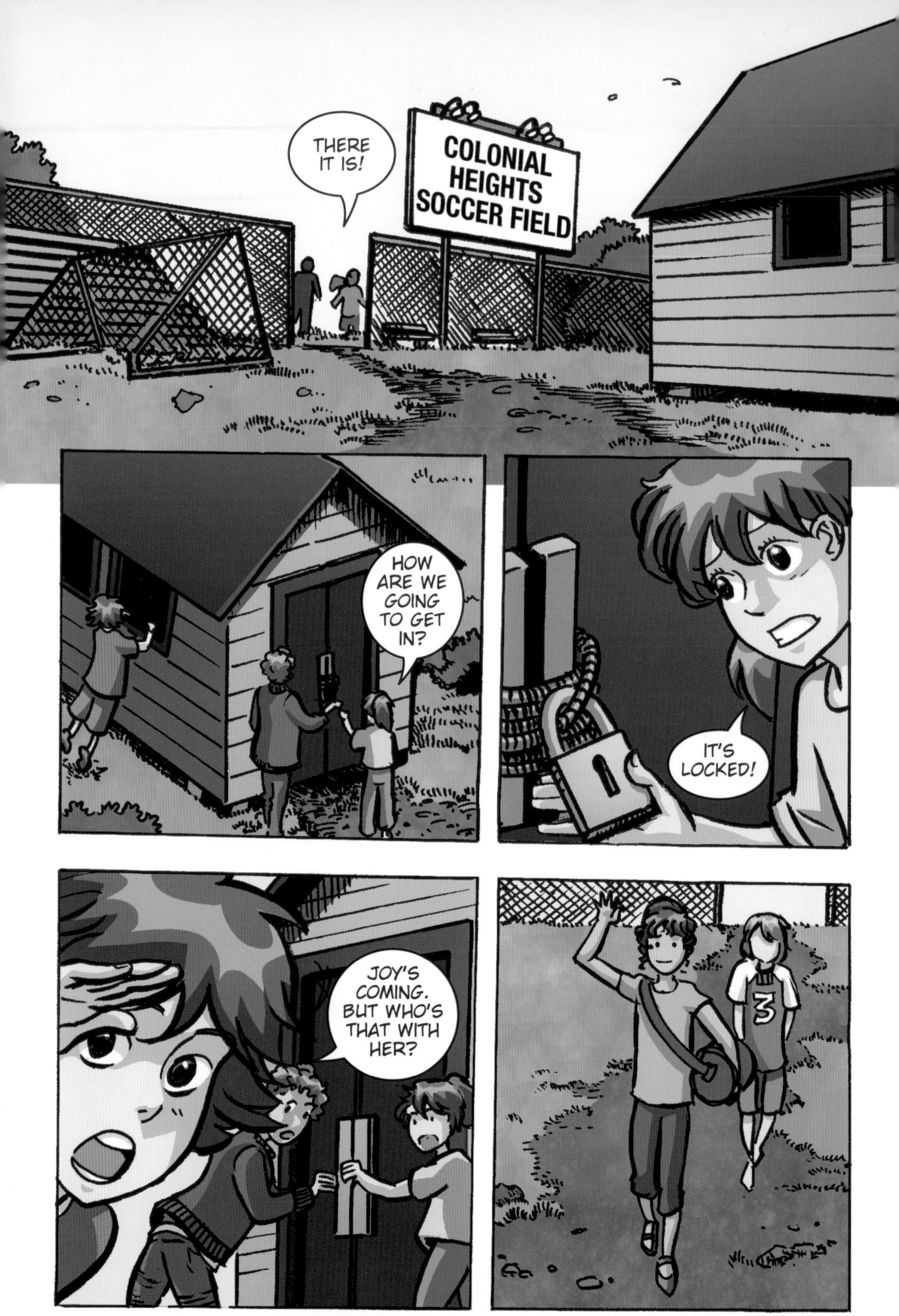
THERE IT IS!
COLONIAL HEIGHTS SOCCER FIELD
HOW ARE WE GOING TO GET IN?
IT'S LOCKED!
JOY'S COMING. BUT WHO'S THAT WITH HER?

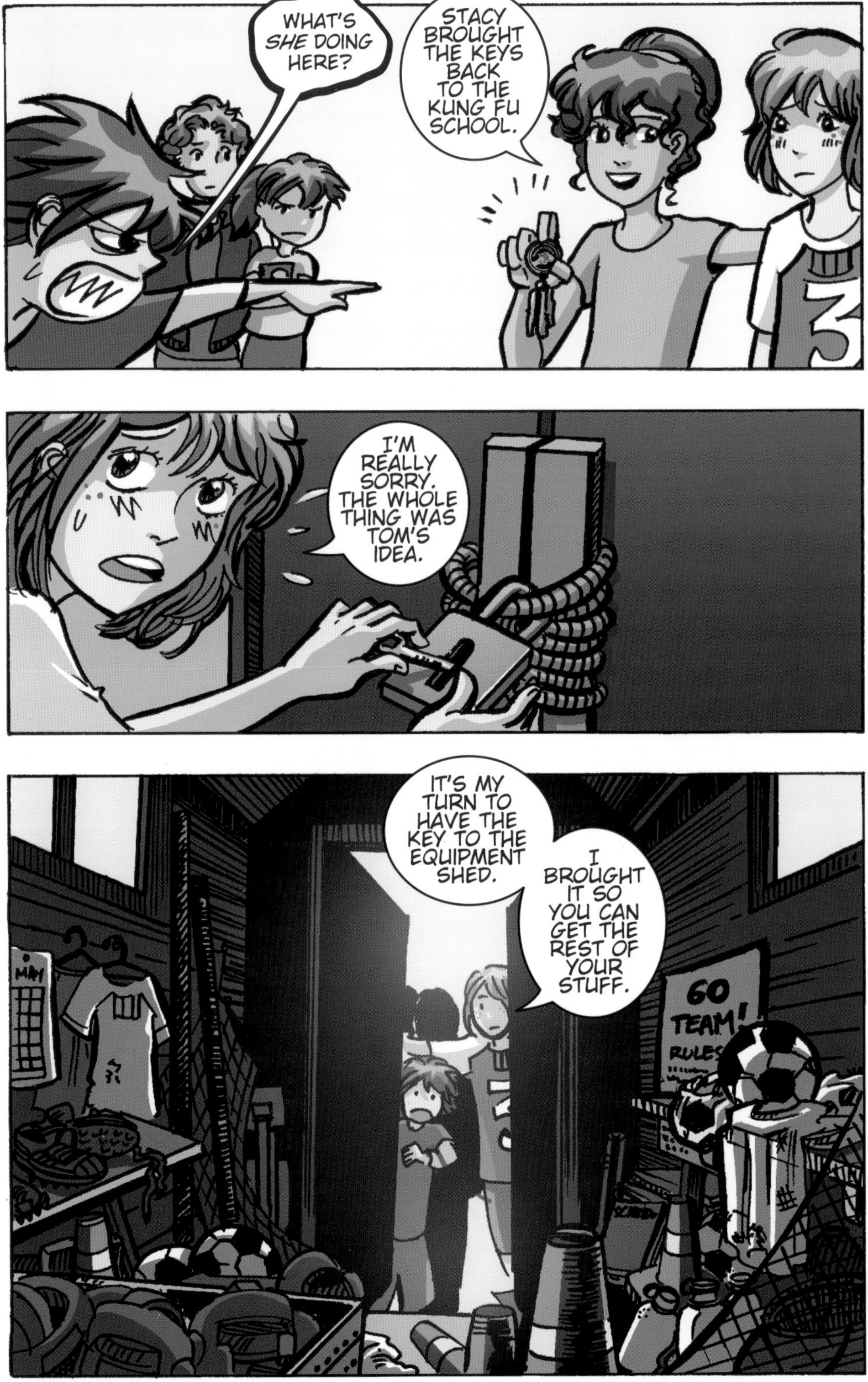

WHAT'S *SHE* DOING HERE?
STACY BROUGHT THE KEYS BACK TO THE KUNG FU SCHOOL.
I'M REALLY SORRY. THE WHOLE THING WAS TOM'S IDEA.
IT'S MY TURN TO HAVE THE KEY TO THE EQUIPMENT SHED.
I BROUGHT IT SO YOU CAN GET THE REST OF YOUR STUFF.
GO TEAM!
RULES

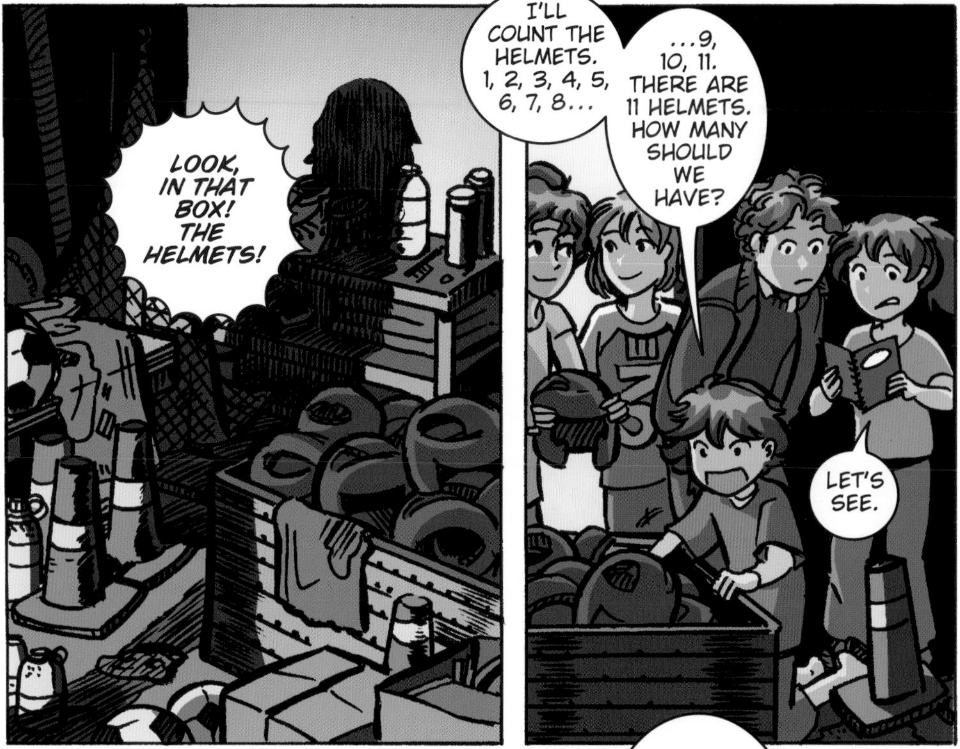
LOOK, IN THAT BOX! THE HELMETS!
I'LL COUNT THE HELMETS. 1, 2, 3, 4, 5, 6, 7, 8...
...9, 10, 11. THERE ARE 11 HELMETS. HOW MANY SHOULD WE HAVE?
LET'S SEE.

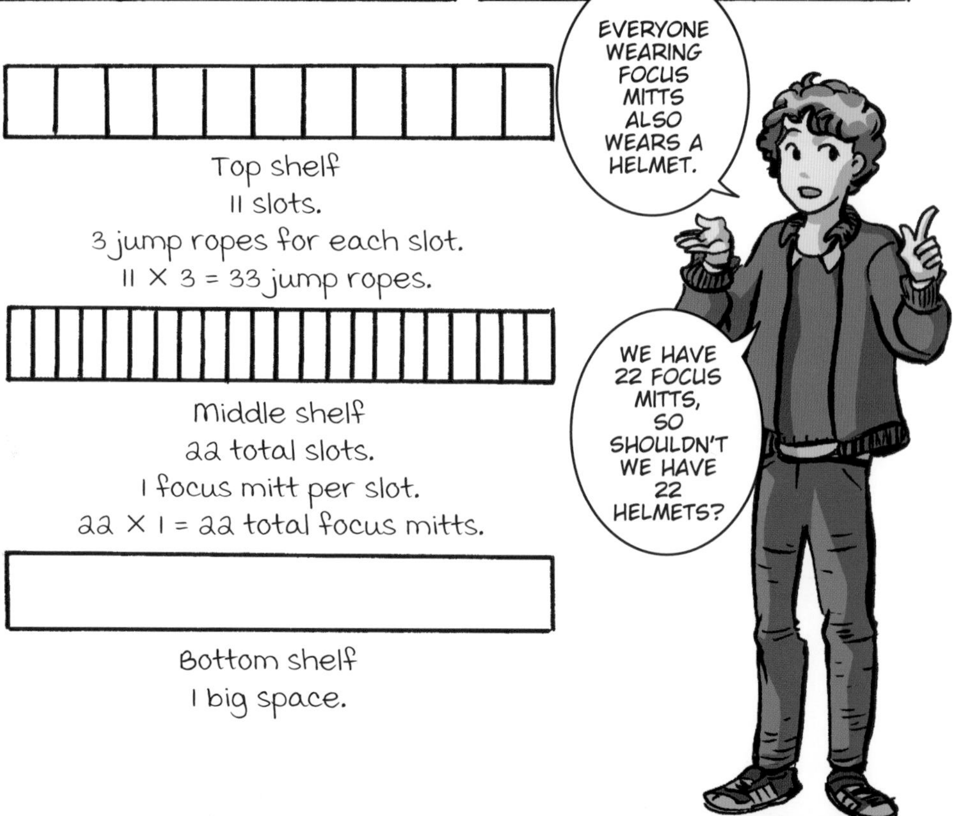
Top shelf
11 slots.
3 jump ropes for each slot.
11 × 3 = 33 jump ropes.
Middle shelf
22 total slots.
1 focus mitt per slot.
22 × 1 = 22 total focus mitts.
Bottom shelf
1 big space.
EVERYONE WEARING FOCUS MITTS ALSO WEARS A HELMET.
WE HAVE 22 FOCUS MITTS, SO SHOULDN'T WE HAVE 22 HELMETS?

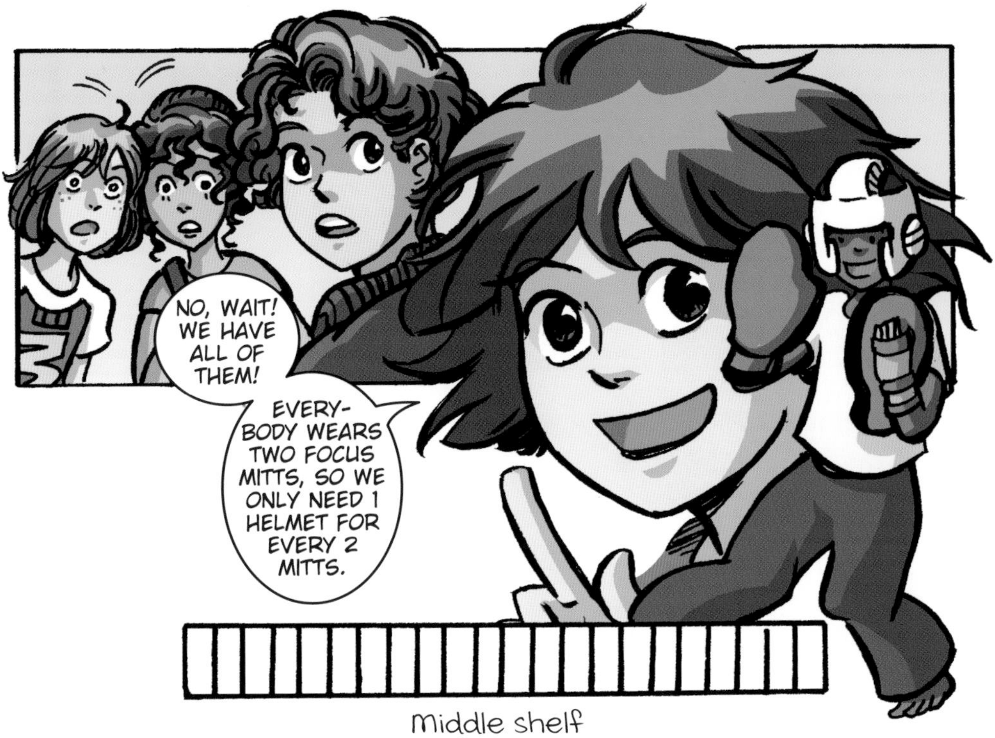
NO, WAIT! WE HAVE ALL OF THEM!
EVERY-BODY WEARS TWO FOCUS MITTS, SO WE ONLY NEED 1 HELMET FOR EVERY 2 MITTS.

Middle shelf
22 total slots.
1 focus mitt per slot.
22 × 1 = 22 total focus mitts.
2 mitts per pair.
22 ÷ 2 = 11 pairs of focus mitts.

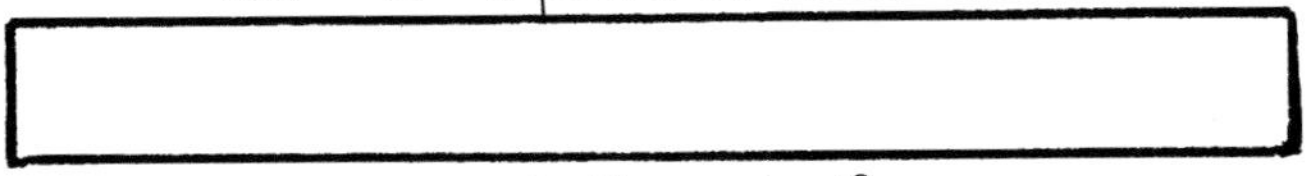

Bottom shelf
1 big space.
1 helmet for each pair of focus mitts.
11 × 1 = 11 helmets.

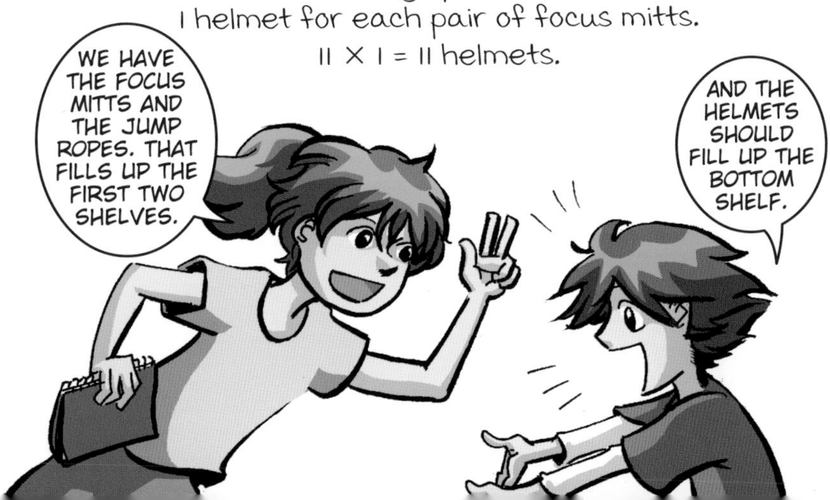
WE HAVE THE FOCUS MITTS AND THE JUMP ROPES. THAT FILLS UP THE FIRST TWO SHELVES.
AND THE HELMETS SHOULD FILL UP THE BOTTOM SHELF.

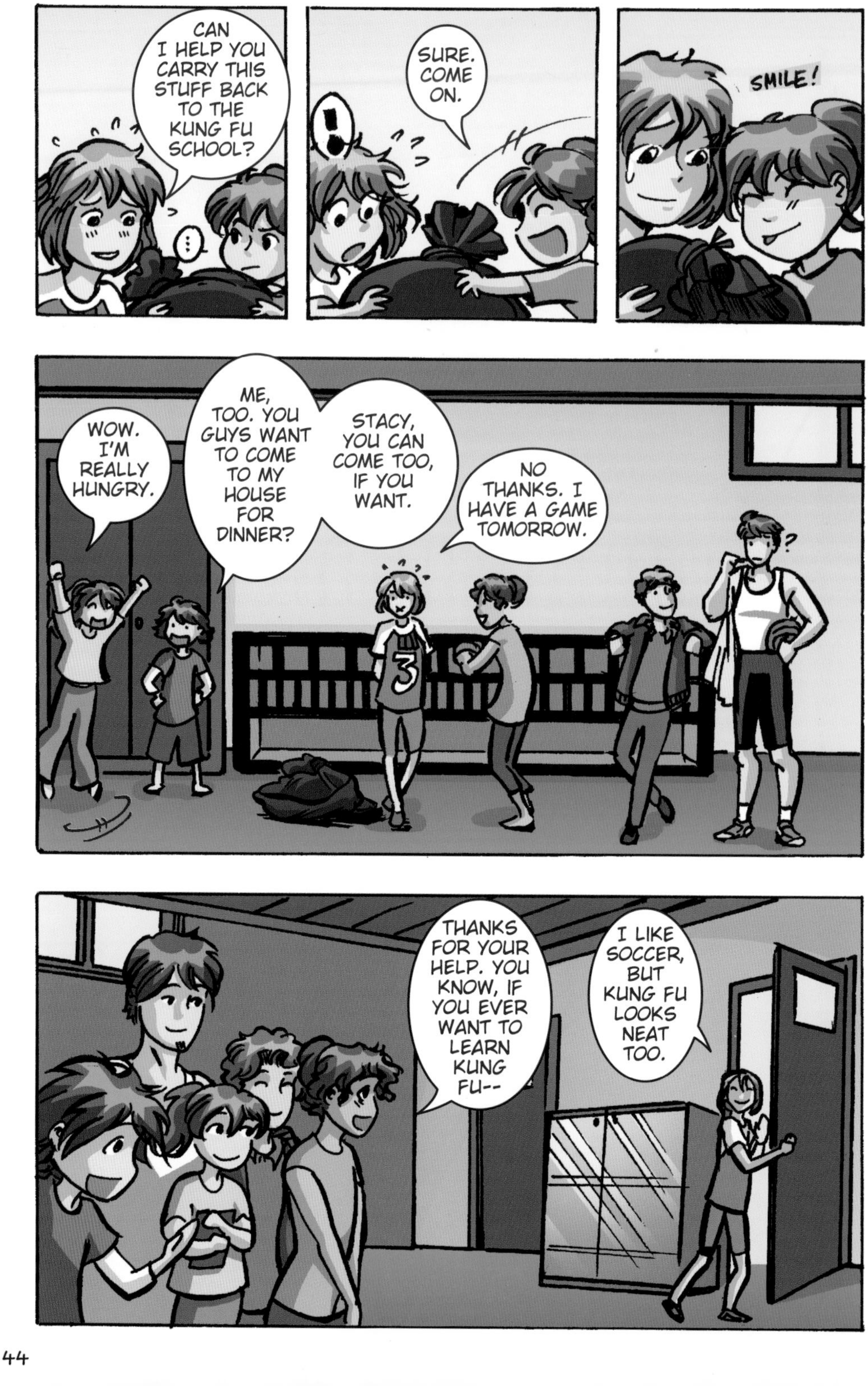
CAN I HELP YOU CARRY THIS STUFF BACK TO THE KUNG FU SCHOOL?
...
!
SURE. COME ON.
SMILE!
WOW. I'M REALLY HUNGRY.
ME, TOO. YOU GUYS WANT TO COME TO MY HOUSE FOR DINNER?
STACY, YOU CAN COME TOO, IF YOU WANT.
NO THANKS. I HAVE A GAME TOMORROW.
THANKS FOR YOUR HELP. YOU KNOW, IF YOU EVER WANT TO LEARN KUNG FU--
I LIKE SOCCER, BUT KUNG FU LOOKS NEAT TOO.

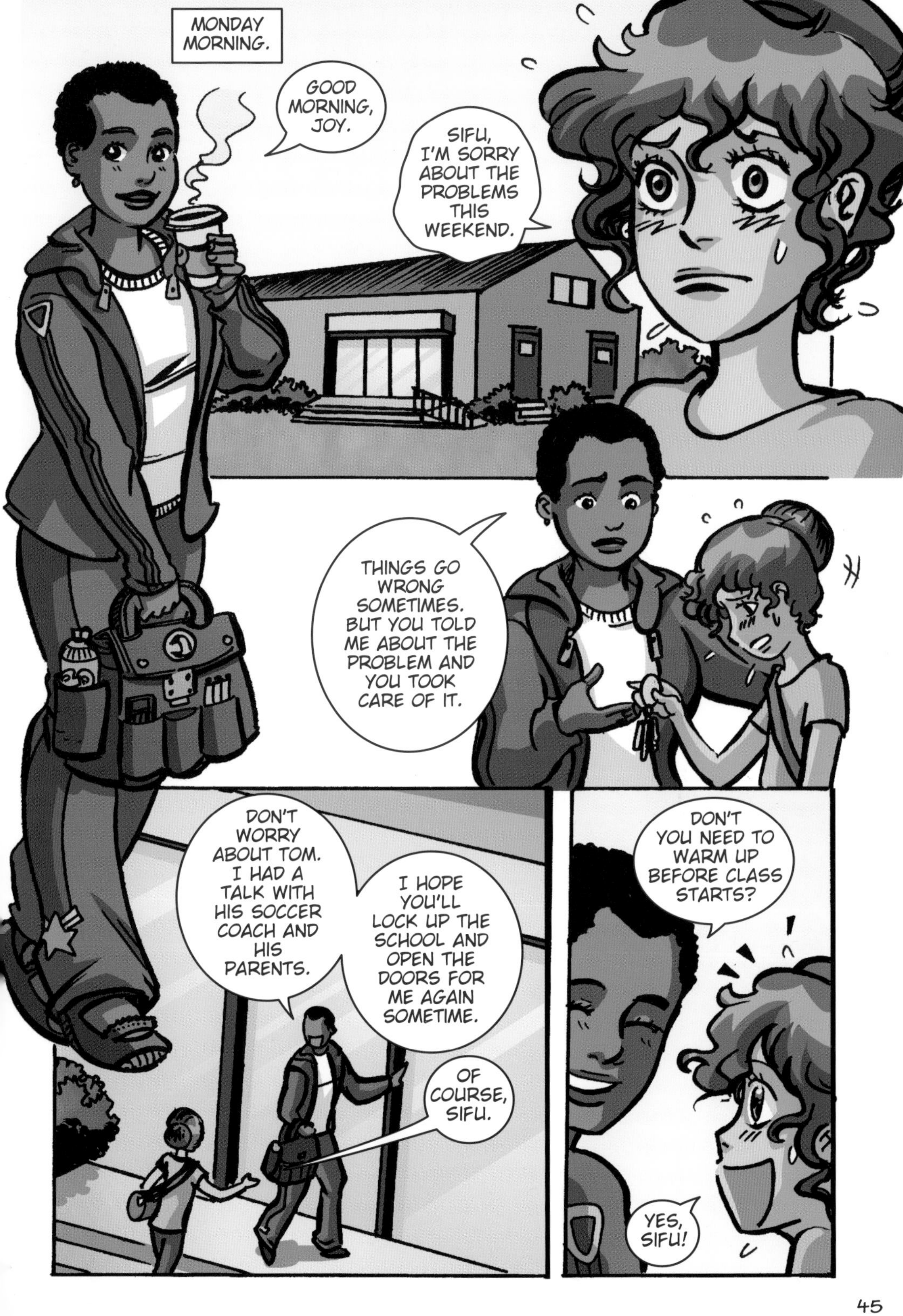
MONDAY MORNING.
GOOD MORNING, JOY.
SIFU, I'M SORRY ABOUT THE PROBLEMS THIS WEEKEND.
THINGS GO WRONG SOMETIMES. BUT YOU TOLD ME ABOUT THE PROBLEM AND YOU TOOK CARE OF IT.
DON'T WORRY ABOUT TOM. I HAD A TALK WITH HIS SOCCER COACH AND HIS PARENTS.
I HOPE YOU'LL LOCK UP THE SCHOOL AND OPEN THE DOORS FOR ME AGAIN SOMETIME.
OF COURSE, SIFU.
DON'T YOU NEED TO WARM UP BEFORE CLASS STARTS?
YES, SIFU!

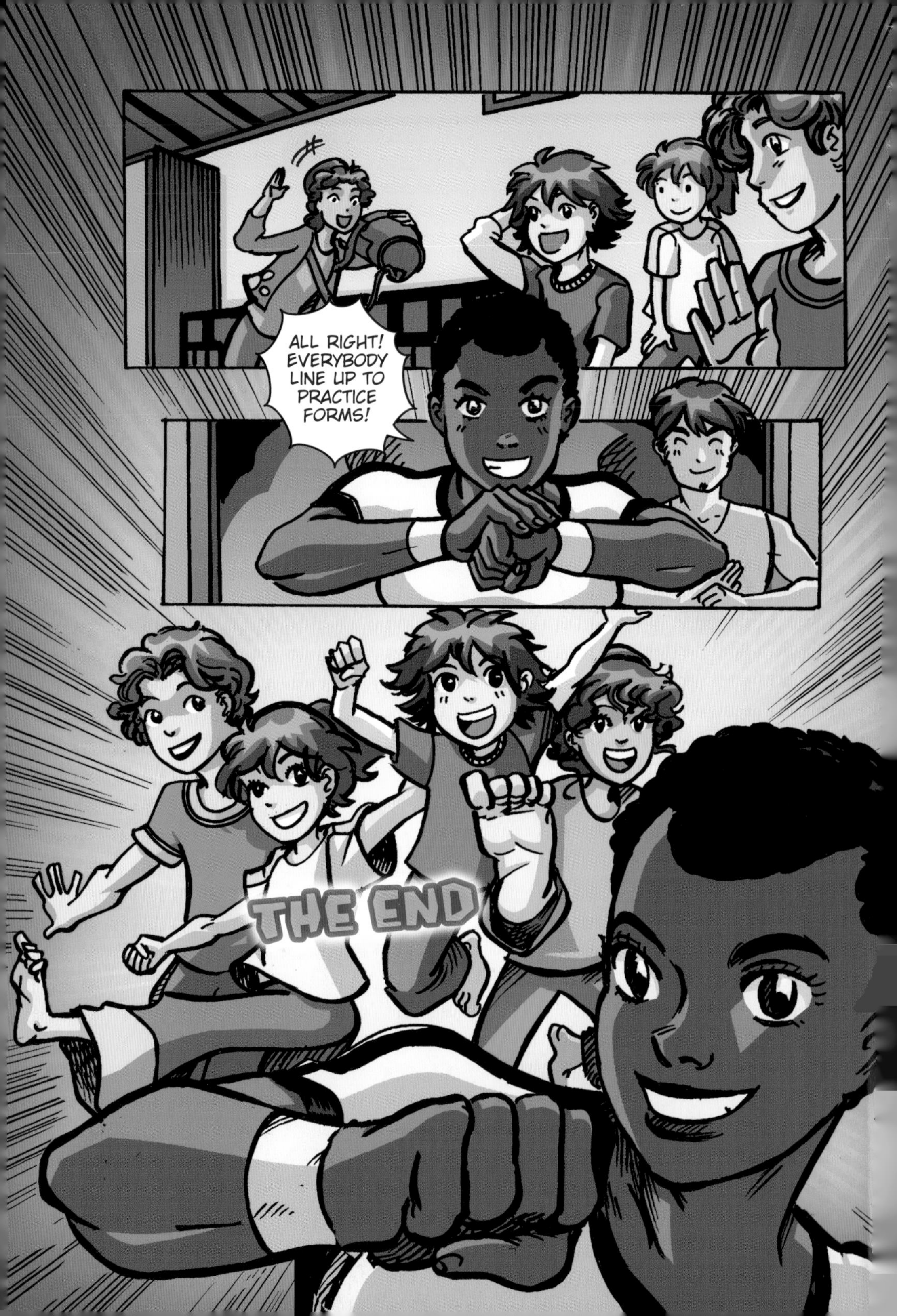
ALL RIGHT! EVERYBODY LINE UP TO PRACTICE FORMS!
THE END

The Author

Melinda Thielbar is a teacher who has written math courses for all ages, from kids to adults. In 2005 Melinda was awarded a VIGRE fellowship at North Carolina State University for PhD candidates "likely to make a strong contribution to education in mathematics." She lives in Raleigh, North Carolina, with her husband, author and video game programmer Richard Dansky, and their two cats.

The Artists

Tintin Pantoja was born in Manila in the Philippines. She received a degree in Illustration and Cartooning from the School of Visual Arts in New York City and was nominated for the Friends of Lulu "Best Newcomer" award. She was also a finalist in Tokyopop's Rising Stars of Manga 5. Her past books include a graphic novel version for kids of Shakespeare's play *Hamlet*.

Yuko Ota graduated from the Rochester Institute of Technology and lives in Maryland. She has worked as an animator and a lab assistant but is happiest drawing creatures and inventing worlds. She likes strong tea, the smell of new tires, and polydactyl cats (cats with extra toes!). She doesn't have any pets, but she has seven houseplants named Blue, Wolf, Charlene, Charlie, Roberto, Steven, and Doris.

Der-shing Helmer graduated with a degree in Biology from UC Berkeley, where she played with snakes and lizards all summer long. She is working toward becoming a biology teacher. When she is not tutoring kids, she likes to create art, especially comics. Her best friends are her two pet geckoes (Smeg and Jerry), her king snake (Clarice), and the chinchilla that lives next door.

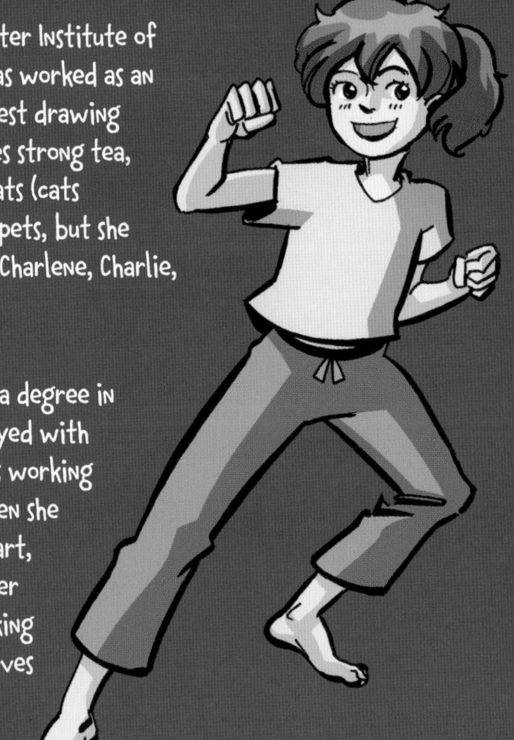

AMY BY TINTIN

START READING FROM THE OTHER SIDE OF THE BOOK!

This page would be the first page of a manga from Japan. This is because written Japanese is read from the right side of the page to the left side of the page.

English is read from left to right, so this is the last page of this Manga Math Mystery. If you read the end of the book first, you'll spoil the mystery! Turn the book over so you can start on the first page. Then find the clues to the mystery with Sam, Joy, Amy, and Adam!

MANGA MATH MYSTERIES #2

Somebody has stolen money from the soccer team. Everyone thinks Tom, the team's big bully, did it, but he says it wasn't him. Should Adam, Amy, Joy, and Sam believe him and help? They will have to figure out how much money was stolen—and also why! The kids work with dollars and cents to find . . .

The Hundred-Dollar Robber

MANGA MATH MYSTERIES

#1 THE LOST KEY A Mystery with Whole Numbers

#2 THE HUNDRED-DOLLAR ROBBER A Mystery with Money

#3 THE SECRET GHOST A Mystery with Distance and Measurement

#4 THE KUNG FU PUZZLE A Mystery with Time and Temperature

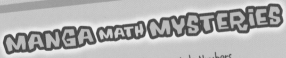